ALSO BY PRU SCHUYLER

NIGHTHAWKS SERIES

Find Me in the Rain

Find Me on the Ice

Find Me Under the Stars

Not My Coach (Novella)

Find Me in the Fire

MRS. CLAUS STANDALONE DUET

Stealing Mrs. Claus

Becoming Mrs. Claus

HEAU HOCKEY LEGENDS SERIES

Saving the Beast

SAINT ELDRITCH SERIES

Shut Up and Bite Me

THE WICKED TRILOGY

The Wicked Truth

The Wicked Love

The Wicked Ending

SHUT UP
and bite me

PRU SCHUYLER

Copyright © 2024 by Pru Schuyler

All rights reserved.

Cover Designer: Jessica @Jesslynndraws

Interior Design: Pru Schuyler

Editor: Sandra @ One Love Editing, www.oneloveediting.com

No part of this book may be reproduced in any form or by any electronic or mechanical means, including information storage and retrieval systems, without written permission from the author, except for the use of brief quotations in a book review.

This book is a work of fiction. Names, characters, places, and incidents either are products of the author's imagination or are used fictitiously. Any resemblance to actual persons, living or dead, events, or locales is entirely coincidental.

SHUT UP
and bite me

PRU SCHUYLER

For those who love hoa hoa season
as much as I do.

Prologue
vivian

For centuries, humans have created tall tales about fanged creatures that are damned to the shadows of the night, but they were wrong—we are most definitely not damned, and we happen to *love* the light.

Most clichés and superstitions about us were created…well, by us as a form of false security for the humans. If they believe we can't go in the sun, then they will never suspect us walking beside them during the day. Besides, it's not our fault that humans love a good story, and we love to tell one.

I suppose not everything written about us is a lie. We do, in fact, survive on human blood, but at least we are humane about how we feed. We only take blood from the willing. *Enough to sustain, never drain.* It's a rule, a mantra, a guideline, or rather an understanding between us.

I can't promise that we all used to do it this way because I know that we haven't, and we also don't need to feed constantly like the movies and books will tell you. In fact, we only need to feed twice a year, unless we are injured or hurt in some way; then, we may require a little blood boost.

We don't go hunting in the shadows or lurk in a dark alley waiting for an unsuspecting victim. Instead, we have an agreement. We call it the Culling, an arrangement of sorts between humans and ourselves.

We've gone by many names since the dawn of time, striking fear in those who speak them—bloodsucker, undead, monster, parasite, demon, and the most commonly known one...*vampire*.

Chapter One
greyson

I'm fine.

Everything's fucking *fine*.

But I'm starting to think that might actually be the problem. I'm tired of the same routine *every single* day. Wake up. Shower. Gym. School. Homework. Run. Bed. Repeat.

Over and over and over and over and over again.

Most of my life has been normal, boring, and predictable, and I used to love every single unexciting moment. I liked waking up knowing exactly what I had to look forward to.

I think a lot of that has to do with my early childhood. The unpredictability of my early years formed the stability I craved later in life.

Being in the foster care system until I was eighteen taught me many things. It taught me that not all people who pretend to be angels are good, and promises are often empty words. I moved around constantly as a kid, bouncing from home to home. Some weren't that terrible, and some were born from nightmares.

Oftentimes, food was used as a weapon and an enforcing tool. There were times I spent days without eating as their form of punishment, or where I was only fed canned dog food for a week because I was behaving like a "rabid animal." Mind you, my "rabid behavior" was leaving toys out after I was done playing with them. To be honest, I think those foster parents never truly wanted to help kids rather than be handed a human punching bag and a check.

If it were up to me, those homes and those "parents" would be burned to the ground. I was forced to learn at a very young age that no one in this world is looking out for me, and the only person who can protect me is myself. Learning on my feet was a skill I quickly acquired.

Shortly after living in my first abusive foster home, I learned to stash food any and every chance I got. If I got a treat at school, I would tuck it into my pocket to save and take home for a time when I would need it.

That was one of many things I would come to realize about the real world we live in. I became so closed off and guarded that when I moved into my final foster home at sixteen, under the guardianship of a sweet elderly woman named Cheryl, I didn't know how to relax, and I didn't know how to trust her.

She bathed me in compliments and promises, and I didn't believe a single one of them. I couldn't. It would be like setting myself up for failure when she would inevitably turn on me.

But over the course of my first year with her, she earned my trust. She showed me I could just be a kid in her home. I could relax and switch out of fight or flight mode. I didn't have to keep secret stashes of food; I could go into the pantry whenever I pleased. For the first time in years, I didn't have to sleep with one eye open.

There wasn't a lock on my bedroom door to keep me inside until she decided she was ready to tolerate me for the day. I was free to move about the house when I wanted.

She was the greatest person I've ever known and ever will. Since she came into my life, I've wanted to do better and be better. I want to be successful and make her proud. Even if she's no longer alive to see it.

She picked up this tattered and cruel teenage boy from the dark trenches where the world spit him out and saw through the anger and coldness. Cheryl was selfless, kind, and generous to a fault. I know that without her, my life would look drastically different.

But because of her, and only her, I'm finishing up my last year at Saint Eldritch University. She would have loved to see this, to see the dreams we imagined together coming true.

The beautiful and foggy Saint Eldritch is tucked away in the deep pine forests of Massachusetts, the nearest town of significant size being over two hours away. So, thankfully, they have everything I could need.

The shops and homes all have unique designs with character, and no expense seems to have been spared for their architecture. Trees decorate the land, lining the dark concrete sidewalks. Everywhere you look, something new is there to mesmerize you. Sometimes this place seems too good to be true. Too *perfect*. In my defense, anything I've ever experienced that was too good to be true ends up being just that.

This town has been my home for the last six

years, two spent with Cheryl and three and a half in dorm rooms and eventually an apartment.

After Cheryl passed, I was all alone with two thousand dollars to my name. All I had were the dreams we discussed together—I would go to school, get a reliable job, and focus on the good in the world instead of always dwelling on the bad. Which is exactly what I've done since we said goodbye. Nothing will stand in my way of honoring her and the plans we made.

The two thousand dollars I had dried up pretty quickly. To make money on the side, I started a part-time job on campus in the library.

After all, reading has always been my true passion, and I dreamed of maybe writing one day. But that was the opposite of reliable income, never knowing if people will be interested in your work. So I pursued finance instead. I don't really enjoy it, but I'm good at it.

As my schoolwork became more demanding, I left my job at the library. I was frugal enough with my money that I've saved up enough to go without a job for my final semester of school, allowing me to focus all of my effort into my studies My goal for myself with a little extra time on my hands is to start running new routes and exploring more during my late-night runs. Typically, I run the same four-mile path every single night. But lately, I've been wanting to try something new.

Some people need constant social interaction to be happy. I, myself, am not one of those people.

Even more so when it comes to my roommate, Steven Johnson. If it wasn't for the lease, I would have moved out the week after I signed it because he's the absolute worst person to live with. He's messy, lazy, selfish, and can't take any accountability if his life depended on it. Aside from running into him in passing, I avoid any interaction because all it does is piss me off.

The second our six-month lease is up, I'm out of there and finding a place of my own. The only reason I even agreed to move in with him was that I was tired of living in the dorms and wanted to save a little money by splitting rent with someone instead of paying it all myself.

I've put up with a lot of his shit over the last couple of months, but today was a breaking point. My day was already shit from almost being taken out via vehicular manslaughter, to dropping my phone into a muddy puddle, and then coming home to a trashed house from him throwing a party in the middle of the day. I tried avoiding it and going into my bedroom in hopes of isolating myself in there, but that panned out horribly because I found a couple passed out in my bed. *Naked.*

Fuck, I swear I've never felt anger pulse hotter in my veins like it did at that moment. I wanted to beat the living fuck out of him for letting people into my room. But I didn't have any energy left and stormed out instead. He was drunk and a mess. I wanted him completely sober when I came back to deal with him.

Who knows when later is going to come, though, because I haven't stopped walking since I slammed my apartment door behind me over two hours ago, traveling the quiet streets of Saint Eldritch.

Running in the evening and nighttime has always been a way to center myself and relax, since I was young. I like feeling the wind blow against my skin and watching the night sky darken and illuminate with stars, the ones we can see in town, at least. It the one thing I have complete control over.

The cool breeze flitters through my long-sleeve flannel button-up, flinging it open and exposing my tan hoodie beneath. Taking a slow and deep inhale, I step through a puddle, my Converses soaking through from the surprising depth of water. *Great.* Add it to the list of shitty things that are happening today.

I'm fine.

Everything's fucking *fine*.

Running my hand down my face, I sigh. I'm tired

of being just fine. I want to be good, great even, ecstatic if that's even possible. I can't tell you the last time I felt adrenaline pulse through my body. I can't tell you the last time I felt *alive* and not like a robot going through its preprogrammed motions.

For a long time, having a *fine* day was the goal in life. Having a day where I ate enough food, drank enough water, and slept in a safe and comfortable bed. It may sound like the bare minimum, but to little dreaming Greyson who slept beneath his bed to avoid the real-life monsters, this was all he ever hoped for.

Guilt rakes down my chest from the mental complaint of my mundane life, knowing that so many others have it worse, including my past self. My palms sweat for taking a decent day for granted.

But that guilt is battling the burning desire for something *more*. Something that makes my heart skip a beat, my lungs sharply inhale. I crave excitement and passion, and for the longest time, those were two things I never knew I could have. But I think I finally realize that I'm well within the means of creating my own adventure. I just need a reason to jump off of the edge and chase it.

"Greyson, is that you?" a voice calls out behind me, sounding vaguely familiar.

Turning my head and peeking around the side of my hood, I spot one of my classmates, Ben Davies.

"Hey, Ben. What's up?" I ask, stopping and turning completely around to face him and his friend walking beside him.

"You alright?" Ben's brows furrow. "Rough night?"

"Is it that obvious?" I chuckle hauntingly, wishing I had shielded my emotions better, a pit deepening in my stomach. I'm usually very good at hiding my thoughts, aside from right now, I suppose.

He nods and thankfully changes the subject. "This is Joey Holmes, my best friend. We're going to grab a drink. Are you heading somewhere?"

Joey extends his hand. "Nice to meet you, man."

I take it, shaking once before releasing it. "You too. And no, I'm just walking, clearing my mind."

Ben walks forward, passing by me without a word as Joey hurriedly catches up. A good ten feet stretch between us as I stay rooted in the cement, and they charge forward a few more feet before Ben spins around with a smirk on his face.

Ben chuckles. "Well, let's go. Clearly, you need a distraction. C'mon, what are friends for?"

Friends.

I don't know if I would consider us friends because we don't see each other outside of class. But he's a cool guy overall, and we joke around in lectures occasionally.

Taking a slow inhale, I force the air out in one quick breath as my heart tries to break through my ribcage.

I'm done playing it safe, and I mean it.

I'm craving excitement like a hunger so deep in the pit of my stomach, in a wretched and dark corner that's never been fed. I'm starving for something more in life, and I'm finally going to take it.

Fuck it.

Stepping forward onto the wet sidewalk, I take a deep breath, the freshest one I have in a long time. "I'm coming."

Chapter Two
vivian

There is something in the air in Saint Eldritch tonight, a feeling that I don't yet understand, and it's putting me on edge, making me feel the need to be extra cautious of my surroundings. On the surface, this town is nothing short of breathtaking. But paranormal secrets hide in plain sight…in the cute shops that tourists flock to, in the bars and restaurants that everyone loves, and in the soul of Saint Eldritch itself. There's an aura of whimsy that draws people here, a mysteriousness that they want to uncover. I've lived here for over one-hundred years and that still holds true.

I've been around long enough that not much

surprises me anymore, but I think that may change tonight. I just don't know why yet. An instinct, a sixth sense, per se—that feeling deep in your gut that's so strong you have no choice but to trust and follow it.

I'm on my way to meet up with two of my friends to celebrate the upcoming Culling, as it's only a day away. Although, we are surely going to do enough celebrating tomorrow night too.

I don't know when this tradition started between Ava, Skylar, and me, but it's become a ritual to party with the humans the night before the event. It's like stepping into their world for a few hours of dancing and drinking while enjoying their company. A reminder of the importance of the Culling and why it even exists in the first place.

Every six months, I, along with the rest of the High Council, host a pairing of humans and vampires. It is always held at my hotel, the Barlowe, and always will be, at least in our district, that is. Twelve districts divide the United States, breaking the large vampire population into manageable factions, each run by a council. They are in charge of their Culling, but it is overseen by the High Council to ensure that the rules are being enforced and followed. As far as districts go, ours is typically the highest desired due to the wealth and opulence that goes into our Culling, no single expense ever spared.

Slowing down before reaching the end of the street, I come to a stop, my hair whooshing forward and wrapping around my face. Long hair isn't always the best friend of a vampire when we're running, especially at the speeds we reach.

"Slowpoke," I murmur, reaching out to my side with my thumb turned down, stopping Skylar as she slams into my hand. "Beat you."

She laughs, shoving my hand away. "Barely."

Running her fingers through her almost pitch-black hair, she tames the snarls and craziness back down as our other friend, Ava, catches up to us.

"There really is no need to go that fast," she pants, and I smirk, wondering how she's out of breath because usually it takes an insane amount of exertion to do that to us, and it doesn't typically happen from running.

"You call *that* fast?" I tease.

Her eyes flick up to mine as she grips the part of her thighs right above her knees with profound strength, the skin stark white between her fingers. "Shut it."

Turning to Skylar, I ask, "Are we ready?"

Lifting the thin straps of her bodysuit up, she shimmies her boobs into place before licking her lips. "Very."

Playfully glaring at her, I murmur, "No biting tonight, Skylar."

"Yes, *mom*, I know," she deadpans, cocking her head to the side.

An arm loops around mine as Ava begins skipping, pulling me along with her. "Let's go. We've already wasted enough time out here."

"We literally have forever," I remind her, happily skipping with her, my black platform boots slapping lightly against the pavement.

Dahlia joins my other side, snaking her arm around mine, and we finish walking the remaining few feet to the front door of tonight's destination—Nightshade.

The bouncer stops us before looking our way, blocking our path with his tree trunk of an arm. "And where do you ladies think you're going?" He faces us as he finishes his question, recognition dancing in his eyes.

He's one of us—Charlie Conway. Although I've never had a conversation more than a few words long with him, I know he's a decent guy, at least…from what I can sense from him. And he most certainly knows who I am.

The way people listen to the words others say to come to a conclusion about who they are, I use a special sense of my own, one that allows me to know exactly *what* they are feeling. I can sense if they are being genuine or deceitful, happy or sad, turned on or turned off, and everything in between.

Thankfully, over the years, I have learned to control it enough to tuck it away until I choose to let it come out to play. When I first turned and discovered I could do this, it was incredibly overwhelming. I wouldn't just feel my emotions; I would feel everyone else's as if they were mine too. And it wouldn't be just one person; it would be a room full all at once. It was agonizing. I couldn't shut it off, I couldn't get a break from it, and it took me nearly two years to get under control. The longest two damn years of my life.

Now, that gift reminds me of an onion. If I choose, I can open myself to anyone. I can peel back another layer and sense what they are feeling without feeling it myself.

If I want a deeper connection, I can allow the feelings in, let them run through my body and race through my heart, let them become my own. It can be intoxicating at times, like a drug where I want to chase the next burst of euphoria. But I haven't used it like a game in a very, very long time.

Besides, my emotions are often more than enough to deal with without involving someone else, so I typically keep that solid brick wall sky-high to block out everyone else's mood swings.

"Good evening, Ms. Barlowe." Charlie dips his head down ever so slightly. "A pleasure as always. You ladies have a good night."

"I'm sure we will." I smile up at him as he pulls the door open, music pouring out of the place, along with puffs of fog from the machines. "Stay out of trouble."

"Always do," he retorts as the black door seals shut behind us.

The inside of this place is packed tonight. No wonder the line outside wrapped down the street and around the sidewalk.

Music pulses through the speakers as we make our way through the crowd to the bar to get a drink. If it weren't for the fact that I have super strength, speed, and senses that make me feel fearless, I would never come in here. This place would be terrifying to me as a human.

We take turns ordering our drinks, and I turn around and lean back against the counter as we wait, scanning the crowd for any familiar faces, at least the ones I can see from here.

Alcohol alone doesn't really do anything to us, and the only time it does is if we consume enough to kill an elephant. However, if we take a little Deadly Nightshade, also known as Belladonna, not enough to do any real damage but enough to weaken our systems a hair, then the alcohol hits us a hell of a lot faster. Which is why before we left my place tonight, we each took a low dose of Nightshade flowers.

Ava hands me my drink, and I take a sip of the vodka soda, trying not to show the disgust on my face, but I fail miserably. *Ugh.* The entire mouthful was basically just vodka, which I suppose serves the purpose of the drink, but it tastes like shit.

Ava and Skylar fall into a conversation, speaking in a normal tone that is completely drowned out by the noise, but not to us if we listen intently enough. But I don't care to eavesdrop on their hot-or-not listing of the guys in the club.

The hairs on the back of my neck rise, and that same eerie sensation from earlier trickles down my spine like a slithering snake. *What the hell is that? Annoyance.*

It's like I'm feeling someone else's emotion, like it's breaking through my barriers without my consent. Which should be impossible.

I hate feeling any ounce out of control, and this is making me feel like a puppet in someone else's game. Curiosity kills the cat, right? Well, it also kills cute vampires named Vivian because I can't ever seem to help myself.

"Look, man, I'm sure he didn't mean anything by it."

Who the hell said that?

Perking up and standing up taller, I open myself to the group, searching for the source of concern. As I bounce between each person I tap into their emotions, the majority are feeling horny and/or annoyed, not what I'm looking for.

"We don't want any trouble." *Where did that come from?*

I hear the same voice again, the tone clear as day, as if he's standing right beside me. But no one is.

Latching onto the voice, I close my eyes and focus on where it came from. I don't know how to explain it other than it's like a string connecting me to whoever I'm tuned in to, and I have to mentally tug on it until I find its origin.

His breathing fills my ears, each inhale and exhale speeding up, and I swear I can feel his breath fluttering through my hair and warming the side of my cheek.

A tree plants itself across the room where he stands. Long, intertwining roots snake beneath the floor, bursting through the ground under my feet, and I feel him as if we are connected.

The moment I latch onto him, I know exactly where he is, and I'm striding forward, swimming through the sea of people to the source.

In seconds, I reach my destination, and all the air dissipates from my lungs.

I've never felt this pull to someone's emotions before or had the desire to let them in like I do right now. I want to feel what he's feeling like an itch I desperately need to scratch.

He's hot in a sexy nerd type of way. The sharp curve of his jaw ticks as he locks eyes with a guy across from him, but I can't seem to tear my gaze away from his tousled blonde hair and summer pool blue eyes, perfectly framed behind his glasses. He's quite mesmerizing to look at. Beautiful. Like he stepped out of a piece of art. I haven't been entranced by someone like this since…well, since ever.

Taking a deep breath, I let my guard down for him and attempt to carefully let in whatever emotion is coursing through him.

Nervousness. Confusion. Hesitation. A little fear and anger…lots of anger. The kind that is rooted deep in the soul, kept away in the darkest parts of a person, and always begging to be let out.

I wonder if his anger wants to have a playdate with mine.

The other guy gets in his face and blocks my perfect view, and the only things I sense from him are the desire for chaos and the guilt for causing it, which is rather contradictory.

I do not have time for this, though, because I'm dying to know more about the hot six-foot-four blond guy that demanded to be noticed by me.

Closing the few feet remaining between us, I slide my hand across the other guy's chest, drawing his attention to me. His fury quickly morphs into arousal, and I try not to throw up. If only he could physically feel my rejection.

Locking eyes with him, I smile. "Hi," I whisper before standing on my tiptoes, mentally visualizing my next words in his mind and planting them as if they were his own. "Apologize for causing a scene and leave for the rest of the night."

Rocking back on my heels, I watch his shoulders relax before he turns to my hot mystery guy.

"Oh, man. I'm so sorry about all of this. Have a good night," he says calmly before speeding off, beelining it for the exit.

This is another skill I've acquired over a long time and lots and lots of practice. I was a very empathetic human, and that manifested into the ability to sway others' decisions as a vampire.

It began very sporadically, but once I realized that in order to have successful recipients, I had to tap into their emotions like I do when I want to sense and feel them, I caught on quickly. It gets me past their walls, and I place my words in their consciousness as if they thought of them themselves. And they never know the difference.

The music dies out between songs, and thankfully, the next one isn't as bass heavy, and I can actually hear without using my vampire hearing.

"That was incredible," the sexy reason I'm over here murmurs to me.

Shrugging, I smile. "What can I say? I have a way with words. I'm Vivian, by the way."

He smiles kindly, and I feel his genuineness like sunshine on my skin. "I'm Greyson. It's nice to meet you."

"Greyson, would you like to dance with me?" I ask him softly, not using any specially enhanced encouraging words to sway his decision. I want to know the truth.

His sweet smile stretches across his face as his heart races with excitement, the blood pounding in my ears, and attraction exudes from his every pore. He likes me. *Good.*

The smooth tone of his words drips with sweetness as he says, "I would love to," and I want to see if the lips speaking them are just as delicious.

Chapter Three
greyson

Vivian's soft hands slide over mine as she presses her back against my chest and guides my hands over her hips, swaying to the sultry music playing around us.

I don't know who the hell this girl is or where she came from, but she is fucking alluring. She rolls her body, the curves of her ass molding against me like puzzle pieces fitting perfectly together.

My hands tighten on her sides, and I don't hesitate to pull her harder into me. I want to feel more of her, *all* of her.

"Fuck." The groan slips past my lips as she looks backward up into my eyes and hooks her hand around my neck. "You are perfect, but you already know that, don't you?"

She smirks and grinds against the front of my joggers, and I can feel every slight movement, my dick throbbing from her touch.

Something about her makes me oddly comfortable, like I've known her forever, even though we just met. And it's making me do things I typically wouldn't have the confidence for.

Skating my hand across the lace of her corset top, I guide my fingers up the center, between her full breasts, and higher until my fingers gently wrap around the soft skin of her neck, her pulse pounding against my grip.

Her eyes darken as she holds my stare and leans into my hand, tightening the pressure on her throat. I take the hint, tightening my grip and pinning her to my chest. Her ass grinds into me harder. *Fuck, she's addicting.*

I don't know what it is about this girl. This is the craziest shit I've ever done. But that's kind of the point. To take risks and push myself from my comfort zone. Maybe she just found me on the perfect night when I've thrown caution to the wind, ready to embrace adventure with my arms wide open.

In sync, we move like water, flowing to the music

as we become one beneath the flashing lights, our breathing syncing together as it shallows out.

My heart is racing, beating in my chest like a bat out of hell. God, I haven't felt this alive in years. And that's sad when all I'm doing is dancing with a beautiful woman.

The song begins to come to an end, but I don't care. You would have to drag me away from her right now.

Especially after today. I need this. I need her. I need whatever distraction from my shitty life she is willing to give me. I'd be honored to be a blip in her day for her to be everything in mine.

Another song thrums in the air, sensual and palpable, matching the passion growing between us, sparking like the fuse on a bomb.

Licking my lips, I lean down, fighting the urge to finally find out what those pretty red lips taste like.

Her lust-blown pupils lock onto mine as she smirks. "You don't need to ask, pretty boy. Kiss me already."

Her words are the undoing of my restraint, and in one swift movement, I spin her around in my arms, slide my hand around her jaw into her hair, tilt her head up, and seal my lips against hers, breathing her in like it's the last breath I'll ever take.

Oh fuck. She tastes like tempting sin and sweet

salvation, and I'm torn between kissing her like an angel or a devil. Her tongue sweeps out, parting my lips, greedy to delve into my mouth, and I have my answer.

Her fingers fist my sweatshirt, pulling me tighter against her, and the fever in her kiss makes me feral. My tongue swipes hers, and vodka hits my taste buds. I swear it's the only time it's ever tasted this good; I want to get drunk on her kiss.

Pulling away, she quickly licks my lips, my cock twitching against her lower stomach, and she smiles in response.

She holds my stare, and I'm incapable of looking away as her fingers trail down my abs and hook into the waistband of my sweats. I don't care that we're in the middle of the dance floor right now, surrounded by a hundred people. The only thing I can focus on is how fucking good her fingers feel as they skirt against the now exposed sliver of skin as she lifts my hoodie up ever so slightly.

She leans up on her tiptoes, and her words are a ghost on my lips. "Do you want to fuck me tonight?"

That's forward as hell, knocking me off my axis for a moment before I recenter myself, knowing exactly what my answer is going to be. I've had a handful of one-night stands, but that was a few years ago when I first started college. Since then, I've kept to myself, not wanting to waste someone's time and give them a glimmer of hope for something more. But if that's what she's offering for tonight, then I'll happily take it.

She makes me feel fearless, like she unlocked a side of me I have always kept hidden. A side that doesn't question what he wants; he just takes it because he can.

"All I've been able to think about is how perfect you are going to look while you stretch out for me. All flushed and out of breath. Fuck. I bet the image in my mind pales in comparison to what's under this." I tug at the tight red top with flowy long sleeves.

She gulps hard, her eyes widening with excitement and surprise, like she didn't expect me to go along. "I want you *right* now."

Huffing as a smirk tips one side of my lips up, I brush the pad of my thumb across her plump bottom and lip meet her challenging stare. "Here in front of everyone?"

A speckle of pink dances across her cheeks as she grins and slowly shakes her head. Without a word, she takes my hand in hers and starts walking backward, pulling me along with her, a dangerous gleam in her eyes, reminding me of a warning sign. But it's too late—I'm past the point of no return.

She faces forward, and I let her drag me wherever

the hell she's going. I think I'd follow her off a cliff right now if she led me over the edge.

We maneuver through the crowd and approach the very back, where black curtains hang down from the ceiling to the hard floor. She turns her head enough to flash me a stark white smile before slipping behind them, guiding me along with her, the crushed velvet fabric brushing against me as I pass through them. They sway closed behind us, and the air seems to electrify in our separate little world.

Dragging my fingers up her stomach, I push her gently at the waist, guiding her back until her back hits the wall, trapped between my arms, with my forehead hovering above hers and our breath a mix of unspoken desires.

I need to feel her. Every single inch she's willing to give me, I will greedily take.

"You want me to fuck you right here behind this curtain with a room full of people on the other side?" I whisper into her parted lips, and she nods with the most devious grin as music thumps, vibrating in the floor beneath our feet. "How did I get so lucky tonight?"

She wraps her right hand around my biceps, her fingers trailing down my arm until her hand overlaps with mine. With her bottom lip tucked between her teeth, she slides my palm down over her breasts, past her stomach, and between the part of her legs, lifting my hand just enough to slip beneath her black skirt.

Her breath quickens, and she pulls her hand away, leaving me in charge. My firm fingers drag up her inner thigh until I reach the lace of her panties hidden under pantyhose.

Her eyes flutter shut, but with my other hand, I catch her jaw and tilt her head back, forcing her gaze to lock onto mine. I hold them with my stare, wanting to look into those swirling hazel eyes while I touch her sweet pussy for the first time.

"Do you care about these?" I ask, tugging on the pantyhose pressed tightly against her center.

She shakes her head, biting harshly on her bottom lip.

"Good," I answer, dropping my other hand between us and tearing the pantyhose apart at the seam that runs between her legs.

Sliding my finger along the edge of the lace, I lift them from her delicate core, pulling them to the side and securing them in place with my other hand as a shiver dances through her body.

Running my fingers through her center, I can't help the filthy smile that tugs at my lips. "Already this soaking wet for me, huh? *Fuck*, I really am a lucky man tonight."

She inches forward, sliding her arms around my

neck. "This night is just getting started," she whimpers against my parted lips.

As I circle my thumb over her clit, her mouth forms the most perfect O. Gently, I ease my finger into her, watching her mouth fall further open and her eyebrows lift as I slide in a second one. Her eyes darken, and from the little light shining behind these curtains, I can see just how badly she wants this, wants *me*.

Resting my thumb against her clit, I draw my fingers back before gently hooking them inside her and thrusting them back in her pretty little pussy, rubbing circles with my thumb until she becomes a sexy mess in my arms.

"Oh, *shit*," she groans into my mouth as her fists tighten, my tan sweatshirt clenched between her knuckles.

My cock throbs, twitching hard against my boxers as I finger fuck her incessantly while showing her clit the attention it deserves.

"*Oh my god*, Greyson, you're actually going to make me—" she gasps as her back arches, her core tightening around my fingers as her first orgasm of the night rocks through her in pulsing waves.

Her face lifts, those perfect lips parting in a delicious O, begging to be kissed as her eyes struggle to stay open.

Memorizing every detail of her as she comes apart on my fingers, I can't help but praise her. "That's it, baby. Fuck, you're so pretty when you come."

As her breathing slows, she throws her arms around my neck and crashes her lips into mine, a new level of passion igniting between us, and I'm never going to get enough of it.

Her body melts against mine, reminding me just how good we fit together as my hands find her waist and my fingertips dig into her skin.

"You still want more?" I ask her, praying to anyone and anything that will listen for her to say yes.

She pulls away and looks me dead in the eyes, fire burning in her stare as she groans, "I *need* it."

Her hands drift to my pants, and her delicate fingers dip beneath the waistband, sliding down my rock-hard length.

"*Shit*. I *really* need it now," she whimpers, licking her lips as she runs her hand up and down, making my eyes roll to the back of my head.

"Fuckkkk," I groan as she slips her fingers beneath my boxers and wraps her hand around me, lifting my dick from my pants and pumping me from base to tip.

"Shit," Vivian mutters harshly, definitely not in

the tone I want to hear right now, and she releases me from her tantalizing grasp.

My eyes fly open, and I rush to cover myself and her, pressing her into the wall while looking around to see if we've been busted. But there's no one there.

"Are you okay?" I ask her, trying to read her face, which has morphed from delicious pleasure to annoyance and anger.

She grabs my chin and quickly kisses my lips. "Oh, Greyson. I wish we had more time tonight. But I have to go. I'm so, *so* sorry. *Trust me*, I would much rather have you fucking me against this wall than be leaving. But I don't have a choice."

Tucking myself back into my pants, I sigh. I'm so fucking confused. "Wait—what? Why? Did I do something wrong?"

She shakes her head, genuine sadness sinking into her eyes. "Not at all. You were perfect. Goodbye, Greyson."

She looks to her right, and I turn to see what she's looking at, but again…there's no one there.

"I don't understand. Is everything oka—" My words fall to the wayside as I turn back to face her, but she's somehow already gone, or rather…*vanished*.

Focusing has never been an issue of mine…until right this moment when I'm trying to study for class, and all I can possibly think about is the girl from the club last night. Thank god I agreed to go with them, or I never would have met her.

Vivian.

I've said her name so many times in my mind that I swear I see the outline of those six letters when I close my eyes.

Regardless of what did and didn't happen with her, nothing's going to be the same. She may never realize it, and I may never see her again, but she changed something in me last night, cutting a leash I wasn't even aware I was tied to. She set me free. From my own boundaries and reservations.

I've got to find her, or at least try. I've got to do something. Even if the only thing I can do is thank her.

"No, it's like an entire room full of like the richest people. I'm totally doing it." Some girl's voice pulls me from my thoughts as I incessantly tap my pen against my notebook, eavesdropping on their conversation.

"You basically just have to be a butler for a rich person for two weeks, and you leave with a life-changing kind of money. There's no way I'm passing this up. I'll scrub their floors with a toothbrush if they ask. I just want the cash."

"Okay, okay, fine. I'm in. When is it?" her friend asks, and I sit up a little straighter in my chair.

Most of my life, I have scrounged up enough money to survive but never thrive. I've dreamed of a life where you buy what you want because you already have what you need. The comfort of not checking your bank account before buying a candy bar in a gas station.

I'll wait hand and foot on some snob for a couple of weeks if it means the rest of my life will forever change.

Listening more intently, I ready my pen and paper for her next answer.

"It's tonight. So you need to make up your mind, like now. We've got to be there no later than 8:00 p.m. Shit, don't let me forget the code word. It's a foreign language, I think. *Mordere me.*" I jot down every word she says, desperate to hear her mention where it's going to be at.

"Sarah, that's crazy, girl." She hesitates for less than a second. "*Fuck it*, I'm in."

Sarah squeals with excitement at her friend's

response. "Thank god. I didn't want to go through this by myself."

They giggle together and whisper something inaudible.

"Yeah, we better hurry, or we're going to be late for the movie," Sarah mutters, and I hear their chairs squeak against the hardwood floor as they're pushed back.

They begin walking away, and I turn to face them, but they don't even acknowledge me and keep on walking. Shit. What should I say? *Hi, I listened to your entire conversation and want to know everything, please.*

They'd call me a creep and run off.

Shit.

My gaze falls to my lap as I sigh in defeat. It was a bit of a pipe dream anyway.

Something catches the corner of my eye, and I turn my head in time to watch a slip of paper float to the ground.

"Hey, you dropped something," I say, rushing to my feet, walking over to the paper on the ground and picking it up. "Excuse me," I say, trying to catch them, but they continue forward like they don't even hear me.

Glancing down at the tattered paper, I see an address, scribbled beneath one word written in large letters—*Culling*.

Chapter Four
vivian

October first, the night of the second bi-annual Culling of the year. Always held on the same date at the same stroke of midnight.

Finally, tonight's the night, and so far, at least, it's going perfectly to plan, and I refuse to let anything tarnish it now. But I'm not going to jinx it just yet; it hasn't truly even begun. My staff has spent the last two weeks preparing my hotel for this very evening, and they did a phenomenal job.

"Sounds great, Harriet. I'll see you shortly," I say, ending the call with Harriet Bailey, one of our council members, as I lean against the cold stone railing of the stairs leading into the Barlowe.

The Barlowe, known for exuding opulence and meeting every dark desire…well, when it comes to interior decor, I mean. The halls, rooms, walls, and soul of the building are carefully dressed in the most delicious shades of red, black, and gold. No expense spared. Although, no expense could have truly been too high for me to afford when this place was built.

Money is such a fickle aspect of this world. You can never have enough, it seems. Your tastes just get richer.

Although, I cannot speak for everyone. I haven't shuddered at the cost of anything for many decades. But I suppose that comes with the territory of being nearly two hundred years old and forever possessing the beauty of a woman only twenty-three years of age.

I have seen a lot in my time, more than I'd like, if I'm being honest. Yet, it is only the beginning of my lifetime. I still have forever to go. Quite literally.

But I don't take my time for granted. I savor every moment possible, especially nights like tonight where all of my hard work comes to fruition.

The High Council exists for the sole purpose of overseeing the Cullings and ensuring that all rules are followed and fairly enforced amongst the vampires. The High Council consists of five members.

Harriet Bailey, thirty-two years old—well, in human-appearing years, or HA, at least. However, she's been thirty-two for the last twelve years. She heads the communication between the lower councils and us, often staying behind the scenes or traveling to the other districts.

Then we have Ava Hart, twenty-nine years old in HA years, which she has been for fifteen years. She is one of the few people in this world I call my friend. She's the one who people go to with concerns and complaints.

Jason Belmoore. Fifty-two HA years old. Seven years as a vampire. He's sweet as sugar and offers a helping hand to anyone in need. He handles our finances and has also auctioneered the last nine Cullings.

Skylar Jane. Eighteen HA years old. She's been eighteen for the last ten years. She's a spitfire who has no issue speaking her mind and reading others' minds. Which is a very valuable skill as our resident sheriff, checking in on the other councils to ensure they are following the rules.

And then there's me. Vivian Barlowe. Twenty-three HA years. I've been twenty-three for the last one hundred and forty birthdays.

My role in the High Council is to observe, oversee, and enforce. I observe the community around us, ensuring that our secret stays a secret, the exception being the humans that participate in the Culling. But they understand the rules of the agreement. If they spread the knowledge of our existence, any money they earn will be taken and they may face more severe consequences. Participating in the Culling is a privilege, one I will quickly revoke to those who don't respect it. I also enforce the rules we have set, dishing out the punishments that are agreed upon by the High Council. Punishing the vampires who have no regard for human life don't deserve my mercy and they don't get it.

Before my twenty-third birthday, I had no idea that the stories of witches, werewolves, and vampires were derived from real life, a lot of them created by the paranormal factions, to hide their truth in plain sight, at least half of it. It's easier to control the narrative if you write it yourself. They filled the stories with lies and superstitions that couldn't have been further from the truth.

Unlike the movies, vampires aren't created through a simple bite. It's far more complicated than that. There is only one way for a human to change and for it to happen, they must be willing.

There is a lot our bite can do. Feeding, sucking

blood from the body, is just the beginning. Our fangs possess venom, each vampire creating its own unique strain. If a human is willing to accept our bite, then we simply inject a lose dose of our venom into their system. Enough to get the job done with the least amount of pain.

But once that's administered, the human must die to fully change. Our bodies still work like before. Our heart beats, blood courses through us, and we seem normal. But we're faster, running quicker than the human eye can keep up with. We become insanely strong. Depending on who we were as humans, we may have manifested a gift, although it's incredibly rare.

On my twenty-third birthday, I was attacked by a man who couldn't take no for an answer. I was attending the theater with a few of my friends. After the show, when we were walking home, we were approached by three men who wanted to take us home and have their way with us. We had no interest, and they had no care. At one point during the attack, I became unconscious and when I came to, my friends were dead. At first, I thought I was too, that I was dreaming when a woman swept me into her arms and asked me if I wanted a second chance at life, one that would last for all eternity. I said yes, and here I am one hundred and seventy-three years later.

It's weird though. It doesn't seem like I've been around that long. It feels like it was yesterday when I became a vampire. As if I blinked a little too hard and time traveled to this moment. I definitely don't feel that old, that's for sure. I feel like I've lived...*maybe* eighty years.

But when your body doesn't age and everyone treats you as you appear, it's easy to live that way. Plus, I don't mind the free drinks when I go out and get hit on.

My dress flies behind me from a strong gust of wind, and shivering goose bumps break across my entire body, stretching from my perfectly styled updo to my black pointed heels.

The air is electric tonight, my skin buzzing beneath the glowing stars and moon. I don't know what it is, but I feel...on edge, like I'm mid-gasp, holding my breath and waiting for whatever it is to come.

"Viv! There you are. You've been missing for like a half hour." I spin and glance up, spotting Ava standing outside of the ten-foot-tall arched doors as she begins descending the stairs to the landing I'm on. "I had to make so many executive decisions, and it was terrible. You know I hate making any and every decision. Ever."

A chuckle escapes my lips, disappearing into the

dark, foggy night. "I know. I'm sorry. I took a call from Harriet and just got lost in my thoughts, I guess."

She squints and furrows her brows, halting in place. "Is everything alright?"

Nodding, I dismiss the sense of unease in the pit of my stomach and begin to ascend the stairs, the red satin of my gown billowing in the wind. "Everything's great. Are we ready for the arrivals?"

Her eyes darken, and a wicked smile tips one side of her lips up. "They already have begun and ended, and might I add, some of them look *extra* delicious."

Rolling my eyes, I hook my arm in hers as the double doors of the front entrance are pulled open for us by my staff.

Security is very important. It is especially of the utmost importance tonight. No human other than those invited may attend the Culling. It is a sacred tradition, and our secrets can never become the public's knowledge. That is the most treasured rule.

Glancing at the large clock tower in the center of the foyer, placed perfectly beneath the sky-high ceiling and dangling Victorian chandeliers, I check the time. Eleven fifteen p.m. The main event begins at midnight. But there is still much to do.

The humans have already all arrived, so now we

are just waiting for our guests. They'll trickle in over the next half an hour, finding their seats in the auditorium hidden beneath the clock tower. Then, the doors will seal shut, and the night will really begin.

Tapping the head of the microphone, I hear the thumps boom in the speakers of the dim and candle-lit circular room. Standing in the center of the stage, I spin around, looking through the tinted glass into each booth on the other side of the dark pane, where the guests have gathered. If it weren't for my enhanced sight, I doubt I would be able to make out a single face.

Once I have acknowledged everyone on the bottom row, I glance up to the second row of booths and do the same, repeating it once more with the third and final row.

My heart is pounding so hard in my chest I'm afraid it might actually burst right here. I've hosted this Culling since the very first one. I have hunted vamps and killed them for breaking our laws. I have faced fear and death itself and won. But speaking in front of a crowd this large always makes me feel so *fragile*. I suppose that's the humanity in me, after all.

"Welcome to the Barlowe," I announce, and light, muffled clapping from behind the glass is heard throughout the circular room. "The night is finally upon us, and I know you are all eager to begin. For those of you who are joining us again, welcome back. We are so happy that you are here. For our newbies in the house, I'll explain how this will work." Lifting my pen into the air, I slowly spin around and show all of the booths. "You have each been given a pen with a red button on the top. The press of that button will signify your bid. You can bid as many times as you'd like, but you can only win once."

I continue. "If an individual piques my interest, I will simply press down on this and speak my bid into the tiny microphone embedded in the side of the device." I demonstrate the motion. "Your bid will then be announced by Jason in the soft-spoken speaker system in each of your booths. If another bid is recognized after yours, you will need to bid again at the higher price to stay in the game. Please, if you have any questions, ask the concierge placed outside each of your rooms. Enjoy your night, have fun—" My tone straightens like a line drawing taut, leaving no room for argument. "And please—" I pause. "—remember the rules."

My heels click against the hardwood circle stage as I make my way to the exit and through the door, passing the microphone off to Jason, who will be calling the auction tonight. He, of course, can bid; he will just have to do it simultaneously. But he's not new to this; he's done it for the last five years.

"Wonderfully done, Vivian," Jason praises as I push open the door into the hallway with a smile on my face.

"Thank you." I grin, stepping through the threshold of the door and making my way to my booth, the one I share with the rest of the High Council.

Ava lightly claps for me as I enter, pride etched in every pore of her perfectly smooth skin. "You did amazing, babes. Seriously."

"Thank you," I coo, sitting down in the empty velvet chair next to hers. "I don't know why I still get so nervous."

"Because public speaking is fucking terrifying." She laughs, and I join in. Our laughter immediately dims when the first human steps onto the stage with a smile and a wave.

He's adorable. Messy brown hair. Looks like he's maybe in his late twenties. He's a cutie. Someone is certainly going to snatch him right up.

He does a fun twirl with a happy grin on his lips.

None of them are required to do anything when they come onstage. There is even an option of a chair if they simply want to sit while the auction takes place. Or they can share a talent, a story, information about themselves, or whatever they desire. It's completely up to them.

It just gives us a little insight into who they are, what they want out of this experience, and depending on what the vamp's interests are, that may sway them one way or another to place a bid.

Jason introduces our first human from the card he filled out when he arrived tonight. "This is Alex. He's twenty-eight years old. He loves to play basketball in his free time and listen to country music. He prefers to date women but has no preference on age or ethnicity."

This earns a few cheers as well as a few boos, which I can't help but giggle at. I'm sure there is someone in here who would love to take Alex home.

Jason continues. "He has type B positive blood and is looking to make this experience a romantic one to remember."

There is no starting bid set, but it is kind of an unwritten rule that you bid high, knowing that your donation is seen by the High Council, and our favor goes a long way in this world. There are lower-level auctions held for vamps of lower income, also overseen by their local councils, all held in different districts on the same night.

Mine, however, is for the filthy rich and wealthy. If you want to participate here, you have to be prepared to dish out hundreds of thousands in the course of an evening to the council and the selected human.

Jason's microphone only plays in the booths; the humans can never hear what he says. We like to keep it that way so there doesn't become a sense of competition to them on who can earn the highest bid. There's enough gossip in the vampire world when it comes to the Culling without adding the human gossip in.

Soft instrumental music lightly sounds in our booth, seeping through the glass of the stage. We play the music to help keep them relaxed and to cancel out any potential noise from us.

The first bid is announced over the speaker, pulling me from my thoughts. "We have five thousand from Juliet."

If there are ever duplicate named attendees, they are addressed by first and last initial. If by chance those are the same, then the full name is read.

"Six thousand for Holland. Do we have seven thousand?"

Jason pauses, waiting for another bid.

"Going once. Going twice. Alex goes to Holland."

We clap, even though only the booths directly beside us can hear. But it's tradition, after all.

Six thousand isn't bad for the first bid. Typically, people hold off bidding at all, wanting to see who the options are first. And thankfully, there's a written rule about the amount that goes to the human.

The vampire's bidding amount is a donation to the local council to use for the good of their community. The bidding amount is never known by the human. The money they receive comes from the vampire themselves, amounting to a minimum of one hundred thousand dollars. They can give as much as they want, but it has to at least meet that requirement.

There are no secrets during the Culling between the vampires and the humans. We both know what we are here for and what benefits exist for both parties.

Vampires can participate in tonight's event, or they can choose a human on their own outside of the Culling, but the arrangement must still be reported to the council by October third, two days following our auction.

For the past one hundred and thirteen years, I have done it that way. I choose someone in need of the funds, and I arrange it outside of the auction, keeping my deals private from wandering, malicious eyes that tend to follow me.

As one of the founding members of the High Council, it comes with its advantages and disadvantages. One of the disadvantages being that everyone else wants to know who I feed off.

They want to target those people for themselves, discover why I choose them, and to be frank, my favor puts them at risk. Not just at risk from the vampires who follow the rules but from the ones who don't, *especially* from them.

My bloodlings don't even enter my home; they haven't for many, many years. Instead, I meet them at various locations during feeding weeks, never the same place twice. Our arrangement is strictly business. No talking. No getting to know one another. I drink, I leave.

Maybe I overestimate my own importance, but I'd rather that than put the human in harm's way for doing me a favor.

The next individual is brought out onstage, a pretty brunette woman. Jason reads her card, and within moments, her bidding is over, and she is replaced by the next human. This cycle repeats itself over and over as a new potential bloodling is introduced and won in the auction by a vampire.

The next hour goes by in a blur of bids and celebrations of pairings. Human after human.

No one piques my interest, although even if they had, I wouldn't have bid. I don't participate in the Cullings. I never have. It's too dangerous for the human.

They may be under my protection for the two-week stay. No one would dare touch them while they were mine. But afterward, when they went back to their normal life, I wouldn't be able to save them from the dangers that would follow. And I know from experience that they would.

Sitting up in my chair, I set my empty wineglass down and anticipate the arrival of the next human to the stage.

The back of my neck tingles, and a shiver runs down my spine as I take a deep breath, every fiber of my being recognizing the delicious scent the second it breaches my nose.

It's intoxicating. Invigorating. It makes every nerve in my body stand on end, begging to be touched. My shoulders shimmy as a shiver runs through them, remembering last night and the hot man behind the curtain.

God, the way he looked at me, the way he touched me…it was like he saw deep inside of me, down to the core. He saw the loneliness, the fire, the rage, every part of me, and pinned me against the wall anyway.

I haven't felt anything like that…ever. I've had my fair share of romance over the years and thoroughly enjoyed my time. When you don't need sleep or to regain your stamina, the options are endless, and I explored almost all of them. Aside from spending time with my vampire friends, I stick to the shadows and the confines of my home.

Last night was unexpected. I should have left him alone, but I couldn't help it. Something deep within me called out to him. I was drawn to him, desperately needing to discover more. Being with him was like touching a live wire, and my entire being jolted back to life. And fuck, I want to feel it again. I was hoping to find him after tonight. I was going to search this entire city, looking for his scent. Every building, every street, every alley. But he found me first.

And in the worst possible place.

Did he know what I was last night when he kissed me? Did he come here searching for me?

"This is Greyson. He loves to play the piano in his spare time and is currently studying finance at the University of Saint Eldritch. He has O negative blood type. He prefers to date women."

Fuck.

Fuck.

Fuck.

Fuck!

"Right out of the gate, we have a bid of five thousand to Claire."

"A bid of seven thousand to Sandra."

"Eight thousand to Samantha. We've got a popular start for Greyson. Is anyone else interested? Oh, wait a second…ten thousand back to Claire."

They continue to bid back and forth until it's up to eighty thousand. My palms are sweating as I hear a woman's name announced with each new bid that isn't my own.

Claire. Sandra. Samantha. It doesn't matter what their names are, they can't have him. My heart is racing, beating in my chest with vigor as I try to talk myself out of what I'm doing.

But it's too late.

Wrapping my sweating fingers around the pen, I lift my thumb, hovering it above the button, take a deep breath, and state my claim, one no one else in this building can come close to competing with. "One million dollars."

The entire building falls completely silent as my bid is announced through the speakers. But that silence is short-lived as every vampire in the vicinity gasps at my participation.

They know as well as I do that I haven't participated in the Culling for decades. My decision may have been hasty and reckless, but I don't care.

The only thing I care about right now is *him*. And there is no chance in hell someone else is going to bring him home. You're mine, Greyson. *Mine.*

Chapter Five
greyson

What in the actual fuck is going on?

It was spontaneous, a complete spur-of-the-moment decision to come here tonight, and I think I may have lost my mind. Because I just walked onto a stage where rich people bid for me, and I must have sold rather quickly because I wasn't out there for very long, I don't think.

Everything about tonight has been *strange*. The security of this creepy but weirdly elegant hotel at the entrance would only allow me in if I knew the passcode, which, thankfully, I had overheard from the girls at that coffee shop.

When I got inside, they escorted me to some ginormous clock that had a secret staircase leading us down to the dark depths beneath the Barlowe.

We each filled out some fact cards about ourselves and even had to include our blood type, which I thought was rather odd, but I suppose that could be a safety measure if we got injured or something. Although it would be even weirder if they had a stash of blood somewhere for that reason.

Then, we had to fill out our information on a contract that I skimmed over. Basically, I would be the winner's servant for two weeks and in return get at least one hundred thousand dollars. It may have been reckless, but once I saw that number, I signed on the dotted line and called it a day.

After that, some hotel staff lined us up and told us to remain quiet while the auction commenced. And everyone was silent, *dead* silent. I wanted to ask a guy next to me if he had done this before, but I got one word out before he shushed me.

By the time I wanted to change my mind, run up those stairs, and never look back, I was being led onto the stage. I couldn't see their faces or hear the people behind the glass, but I could feel their stares like a thousand fingers ghosting across my skin.

After only a minute or so, the exit door opened again, and I walked through, passing the man I had handed my card to. He was ecstatic, the most joyous look upon his face, and I wondered why. But not enough to stay and ask.

What have I gotten myself into? Is this safe? Is it even legal?

I should have asked more questions, thought this through more. But that's always my issue. Sometimes thinking things through just means giving yourself enough time to talk yourself out of it, even if it's the wrong decision.

Besides, it's too late now.

A group of other people that just auctioned themselves and I file into an elevator with one of the staff. Her name tag reads Lana.

The doors seem to close at a record-breakingly slow speed, the mirror reflection forcing me to look straight into my own eyes. It also forces me to see the rest of the elevator, including the girl Lana, who is staring at me so intently that an eerie shiver runs down my spine. And she isn't even attempting to hide it.

"I wonder why she chose you after all of this time," she murmurs, and the whispers of the others fall silent as they listen in.

"I'm sorry?" I ask, clearing my throat.

Lana smiles sweetly. "Ms. Barlowe hasn't participated in the Culling for decades. But then, all of a sudden, she bids on you. It's interesting…" Her hand reaches up, and she runs her pointed nail down my jaw and beneath my chin.

"Wait—are you talking about *Ms. Barlowe?*" someone shrieks excitedly.

Lana simply nods.

A few others express their surprise before one of the guys quiets them down, grabs my shoulders, and spins me around to face the group. "Is this your first time? You seem nervous."

I nod, my heart pounding in my chest. "It is, yeah. You? I'm Greyson, by the way."

He sticks his hand out, and I take it. "My name's Ethan. No, I've been doing this for six years. This will be my seventh." He blows a raspberry. "Your first time and Ms. Barlowe comes out of the shadows for you. That's crazy, man."

My brows furrow. "You know her?"

"Personally? No. But everyone knows *of* her. She owns the Barlowe." He lifts his hand, gesturing to everything around us. "And as long as I've been doing this, she's never even placed a bid."

Lana agrees and looks at everyone with a glare that we should shut up. "He's right. But don't worry. I'm sure she'll take great care of you."

That's the last thing said during the ride up. We stop on each floor, and a few are called off the elevator to join the staff waiting for them. It's so incredibly organized I don't know whether to be impressed or terrified.

It's only me and Ethan left as the elevator climbs to the thirteenth floor.

"Want some advice?" Ethan leans over and whispers into my ear.

Nodding, I'm thankful for any tips on how to navigate the inevitable unknown. "Please."

"If your bite marks take longer than a minute to heal, which they shouldn't, but on the chance that they do, put some Aquaphor on it, and they'll be healed almost instantly."

Wait, what the fuck did he just say?

Bite marks?

Is that like a kink that everyone here has? I'm not too sure about letting some random woman bite me.

The elevator dings, the door opens, and Lana gestures to us to exit. We step into the hallway and are greeted by two guys, each one holding a sign with our name on it.

"Wait, hold up. Ethan," I call out as we are escorted in opposite directions.

He lifts his hand into the air, forming a thumbs-up, and shouts, "You'll do great! Bonus tip—drink pineapple juice. It makes it sweeter for them. See you on the other side, my friend."

What the fuck is going on? Makes *what* sweeter? And sweeter for *who*?

"Greyson, right this way, please," my assigned staff member says, ushering me further down the hallway. "This is your room. Please wait inside, and your chosen will be with you shortly."

"My *chosen*? What does that mean?" I ask, and he looks at me like I'm stupid.

"The individual who won you in the auction. She'll be here soon," he says, opening the hotel room door.

He holds my stare for a moment, and I'm starting to think all of this was a very, *very* bad idea.

"Do you need anything while you wait?" he asks, looking at me in the same way Lana was.

"Someone to tell me what happens next?"

He looks at me once again like I'm completely stupid and should already know the answers. And maybe I should.

Maybe you're not supposed to lie your way into this event. But I'm here now, and it's too late to back out, so maybe I should start faking it. Faking that I actually belong because I want that life-changing money those girls were talking about.

"Sorry, it's just the nerves," I say calmly, walking into the room and sitting down on the bed. "I don't need anything. Thank you."

"Of course. Have a good night." He swiftly closes the hotel room door behind him on his way out.

Taking in the room, I'm once again in awe. It's the nicest place I've ever been in.

This entire evening has been a whirlwind, and I have a feeling it's only the beginning. But I need to know more about what is to come and what the hell Jeremiah meant about bite marks and pineapple juice.

To be honest, if whoever this woman is gives me enough money, she can bite me all day long. Unless it's like a cannibal thing, in which case I'm out.

Lying back on the bed, I stretch my arms out and stare at the black ceiling fan spinning around. The image of Vivian coming in that dark bar flashes in my mind, and fuck, now I don't think it'll ever leave. She disappeared last night before I could get her number, and I might become a regular at that bar if it means a chance to run into her again.

Fuck. She's like sin and salvation tied together with a pretty black bow. And I need more of her, *so* much more.

If she looks that stunning coming from my fingers, I'm dying to see what she looks like coming with my dick buried inside of her.

KNOCK. KNOCK.

Flying up, I sit tall as my finally calmed breathing

speeds back up. Is this her? The seemingly infamous Ms. Barlowe?

I wonder what she'll look like. Will she be kind and nice or a raging bitch? I wonder what chores she'll make me do while I spend the next two weeks with her.

My curious thoughts are pushed to the wayside when the doorknob twists, the door swings open, and my jaw falls to the floor.

Jumping to my feet, I rush over and take her soft hands in mine. "Vivian. What are you doing here? Are you participating in the auction too?"

She scoffs like she's waiting for the punchline. "I don't understand. What are *you* doing here?"

"It's kind of a long story. I'll tell you later. Are you allowed to be in my room? I don't want to get you into trouble." Her attire finally clicks into my brain, and my eyes wander over every inch of her body, and I have to stop myself from drooling. "Holy shit. You look incredible."

She smiles devilishly. "Kiss me."

"W-What?" I stutter, wondering why she doesn't seem to be as on edge about everything going on as I am.

Any humor disappears from her gaze as the look of her in front of me brings me an ounce of peace. "Kiss me, Greyson. Like you mean it."

I have so many questions. What is she doing here? How did she find out about this—

Stop.

For the first time, I stop thinking it through. I just act.

Stepping forward, I slide my hand along her jaw and into her hair, tugging her toward me as I lean down and claim her lips with my own. Her hand falls to my waist, and she bunches the fabric in her fist, pulling us tighter together as my tongue sweeps the seam of her lip, dipping inside of her sweet mouth.

This is what should have been happening all night last night, but I don't care. The fact that she's here at all right now is an insane coincidence, and I don't want to question it. I want to enjoy every second I have with her.

Sliding my hand down her waist, I lightly dig my fingers into her side, and she moans into my mouth.

We move in sync, our mouths and bodies dancing to a rhythm that only we can make. It's like we were born to fit together. I never want this to end. But she gradually pulls away, rolling her forehead against mine as we both catch our breath.

"Should I show you *how much I mean it* again?" I whisper into her parted lips, and a shiver runs through her body as her smile lifts.

Stepping back, she playfully rests her hand against my chest. "Later. We need to talk first."

Rubbing the back of my neck, I glance at the closed door, scared that at any moment, the woman I'm waiting for will walk in here and catch us together.

"You should probably go. I don't want to get you into any trouble with Ms. Barlowe," I say cautiously. I don't care if they kick me out, but I don't want to mess up her chances of getting a ton of money.

She bursts out laughing as she walks over and sits down on the bed, patting the spot next to her. "I'm not worried about that. Trust me."

Sitting down beside her, I lean back on my hands. "Do you know her? Is that why you're here?"

She ignores my questions. "Greyson, were you invited tonight?"

"W-What do you mean?"

She sucks the bottom of her lip between her teeth. "Did you receive a personal invite to the Culling?"

I don't want to lie to her, although, for some reason, I feel like the truth could potentially harm the outcome of my situation. "No. I didn't."

Her eyes squint ever so slightly. "Then how did you get in?"

Scoffing nervously, I tell her the truth. "I overheard a few girls talking about an auction where you are basically just a servant to rich people for two weeks and you make a fuck ton of money. They dropped a paper with the address, and now I'm here in a room waiting for some lady to come in."

She glances down, fighting the smile tugging at her lips. "You thought you were going to be a maid for two weeks?"

I nod.

She smiles humorously. "You were prepared to wait on this person hand and foot?"

I nod again, a pit forming in the bottom of my stomach as my nerves begin to pick back up.

"Why?" She asks one word that seems to have a never-ending answer.

Holding her stare, I take a deep breath as I decide what to say. And I respond honestly, "Because I'm tired of barely getting by."

"Are those the only reasons?" She pushes me for more.

As if she pulls the words from my lips, I tell her the feelings I've kept hidden from even myself. "Because I don't even really feel like I'm alive. I've lived my life making the decisions that I thought I should rather than what I wanted. I want to feel like I matter. Like I exist. And this is the start of that."

"Good to know." She looks up through her lashes

and asks, "So you don't know why you're really here?"

"What do you mean?" My words are a soft whisper.

Reaching out, she runs her thumb along my bottom lip. "You don't know what I am, do you?"

"*What* you are?" I repeat her words as a cold breeze skates across my back.

She slides across the bed, pressing her thigh against mine as she turns into my body, cupping my jaw with her hand. "It might be easier to show you rather than tell you."

My gaze bounces back and forth between her eyes, desperate to learn the information that lurks behind them.

Is she a serial killer? Is that the *what* she was referring to? Is she… I don't know. My mind is running rampant with ideas. But right now, melting beneath her touch, I don't care what she's about to say. I just want her to keep touching me.

"Then show me," I whisper, leaning down and closing some of the distance between our faces.

Slowly, she inches forward, quickly placing a delicate kiss on my lips. "Your world is about to change forever."

Sitting up, she brushes her hair back from her face and closes her eyes. The air seems to chill around us, goose bumps breaking out all over my body from the anticipation, and I sit forward, preparing for anything.

But nothing could have prepared me for *this*.

She opens her eyes, and my mouth instantly dries as I suck in a sharp breath. Long gone are the beautiful hazel depths of her eyes; instead, they are now a deep red. Not the color of a firetruck or an apple but the dark shade of blood.

And then she smiles, and I see them.

Fangs.

She runs her tongue along the sharp, stark white points protruding from her gums, positioned where an animal's canine teeth are. The very two reasons that I'm starting to believe in the stories of monsters and myths.

"Are you scared?" she asks, studying me intently.

I probably should be. I should want to run away and never turn back.

But I won't.

I'm done living life with fear at the forefront of everything I do. I knew something was weird about tonight, but I never would have guessed it would have to do with real-life vampires. I haven't felt more alive than I do right now.

"No," I answer honestly.

"Good," she replies, her shoulders relaxing. "I

know you have a lot of questions. But let me explain a few things first, okay?"

Nodding, I agree. "Okay."

The thought of Ms. Barlowe lingers in the back of my mind, but I shoo it away, not caring who walks in at this point.

She rolls onto her stomach, resting her head on the palms of her hands as she looks up at me. "Do you know what I am?"

I lean back on the bed beside her, turning my head to face her. "I have my suspicions."

"And they are?" She drags out the question like she's unsure if she even wants to ask it.

"You're a vampire."

She smiles softly. "I am. Do you have a better idea of what your role in this is?"

It doesn't take a genius to figure it out—well, as long as the lore is accurate. "That Ms. Barlowe will drink my blood?"

She nods ever so slightly. "Yes. The bi-annual Culling brings together willing humans and vampires. We make a deal. We feed on you for two weeks, and you walk away with a large lump sum of cash."

"Well, at least the cash part is still real," I laugh. "And you said walk away. So she won't…kill me?"

She cackles. "No, *I* won't kill you." She leans back and sticks her hand out between us. "I suppose that I should properly introduce myself. My name is Vivian...*Barlowe*."

Everything falls into place, and it's like the confusing parts of the night are finally clear.

"Barlowe? You're the one they were all talking about? You're the one who bid on me?" I ask, the questions falling from my lips of their own accord.

She glances away, and a look of pain crosses her features, but before I can blink, it's gone, and her gaze is locked back onto mine. "I would love to hear what they were saying. And yes, I'm the one who bid on you."

"Why?" I ask, wondering if this is a dumb thing to ask after what we shared last night.

Her cheeks redden. "Because I'm not a big fan of people touching what's mine."

"Yours?" I chuckle. "Oh, really?"

She looks down into her hands before glancing back up at me, a softness in her hazel eyes, the red gone. "Feeding can be an...*intimate* experience, especially if there is any attraction between the involved parties. It can be intense in the best of ways. And the thought of another person having their hands all over you with their fangs sunk into your neck makes me..." She trails off. "The only option was this. Otherwise, a vampire would be dead on this hotel room floor the second they tried to bite you."

My dick pulses at her possessiveness. I don't know how I'm finding all of this vampire stuff to seem so normal. Maybe if it were anyone but her telling me this, I would be scared and run out. But maybe this is that *something more* I've been searching for my entire life.

I'm not going anywhere.

"I love it when you flirt with me," I tease her, and she smiles.

"You think that's flirting? Oh baby, we're just getting started."

Wind rushes through my hair, and in the blink of an eye, she's straddling me, the slit of her dress hitched onto her side.

Resting my hands on her hips, I brush my thumbs against her dress and exposed skin. "That explains how you disappeared last night. For a minute, I thought I had imagined you."

"Sorry about that. I really didn't want to leave," she murmurs, leaning forward and resting her hands on my chest.

Silence stretches between us, and my mind starts racing with a thousand what-ifs and questions of the unknown. I'll start with this. "Will it hurt?"

She shrugs. "At first. The puncture stings, but it quickly fades. Especially when you're willing to accept the bite. Which you have to be. I won't feed on you without your consent."

"Does it feel differently that way?"

She nods. "For an unwilling human, the pain can be excruciating and never-ending during the feeding. The rejection triggers a venom in our fangs to release into their blood, and that's what hurts them and paralyzes them in place. But it's against our rules to feed on anyone who doesn't want it."

I'll make sure that when that time comes, I am thinking only positive thoughts because I definitely don't want to fucking find out what her venom feels like.

I chuckle. "Vampires have rules?

She rolls her eyes. "There's a lot you don't know about my world, Greyson. Look, I'll tell you everything you want to know. But I want to go home first. Get you settled in, and then you can ask me anything."

"Your home?" I ask.

I didn't realize that this arrangement included staying with "my chosen." Although the idea of being in close proximity to Vivian doesn't sound like too bad of a requirement.

"You will have to live with me for the next two weeks. It's part of the agreement." She opens her mouth again like she has something else to say, but her lips close instead before she adds, "If you're not comfortable with all of this, you can leave. I won't make you do anything you don't want to do."

This is insane and the craziest thing I've ever done. But I've also never felt more *right*. Like this is exactly where I'm supposed to be.

Grabbing her hips, I slide her up until she's positioned against my growing hard-on. I can't help it. The way she feels on top of me...I want her to stay there forever. "Oh, I'm all in. We just have to stop at my apartment first so I can grab some clothes and stuff."

I blink and she's gone, like she teleported across the room. She's now leaning against the wall casually, like she's been waiting on me.

"Are you coming or what?" she asks, biting down on her bottom lip, smiling.

Standing up, I stalk over to her and slide my hand in hers. "One thousand percent."

Opening the door, I let her lead the way as we step through the threshold, and I realize that she was right—my world will never be the same.

Chapter Six
vivian

He didn't run screaming. He didn't try to attack me or drive a stake through my heart. Those are all very positive outcomes from the conversation we just had. It honestly couldn't have gone better, in my opinion.

You might think that immortality would make you more patient, but that is not the case for me.

Greyson has been in his apartment for ten minutes, and it's taking more willpower than I'd like to admit to not go in there after him. But maybe that's my selfishness. I want him in my home, at my whim. Maybe it just has to do with the fact that I'm hungry, starving really, and desperate to taste him.

But also that I know he will be safe inside my home, where no other vampire would dare to enter without my permission.

Closing my eyes, I focus my listening behind his apartment door, my curiosity getting the better of me.

I recognize Greyson's voice immediately. "Steven, I don't have time for your bullshit right now, dude. I need to get going. Eat whatever the fuck you want of my food, although it's not like you've ever asked before. Just please, for the love of god, stay out of my room. It's the only part of this place I care about. Or just go to bed already. It's like 2:00 a.m. right now."

His roommate, Steven, laughs, and based on where his voice is coming from, he's in really close proximity to Greyson. "I'll do my best. Where are you going anyways? Did little Greyson finally get a girlfriend?"

"First of all, nothing about me is little. Secondly, I may have allowed you to walk all over me before, but that's done. Thirdly, it's none of your fucking business. Get out of my way."

"Yeah? Who is she? Is she waiting outside for you? I'd *love* to meet her," he says with disgusting emphasis.

I take this as my cue.

Moving with hyperspeed, I rush into their apartment, race across the room, and stop directly behind his roommate as I lean up on my toes, placing my hands on his shoulders.

"She's right here," I whisper into his ear.

He jumps out of his skin and whips around. "Holy shit! When the fuck did you get in here?" He takes a few calming breaths before looking down the length of my body as a gross smirk lifts his dry, cracked lips. "*You're* Greyson's girlfriend, huh? Don't waste your time on him, baby. Take a ride on me instead."

Holding his stare, I decide instead of that offer, I'll make one of my own.

I feel the power stretching from deep within my core, out from my body and straight into his, wrapping around his mind and sinking into every cell like a chokehold he won't be able to shake loose.

My words are now his command. "Close your mouth and sit on the couch. Five minutes after we leave, you may return to your normal self."

He nods once, blinks hard, and turns, walking toward the couch without a word.

Perfect.

After we're gone, he'll regain control of his mind and go back to normal, not remembering the order I gave him. His mind will convince him that we spoke casually, and then we left.

"Woah. Did you just do some weird voodoo thing?" Greyson whispers, stepping toward me while watching his roommate mindlessly sit down on the couch.

Searching for his emotions, I open that part of myself to him, and what I find is sweet on my tongue. Pride and arousal.

I giggle. "It's not voodoo. It's a *suggestion*, a powerful one at that." His roommate rests his hands in his lap, staring straight ahead blankly. "Don't worry. He'll be fine and won't remember my telling him."

"Okayyy." He drags the word out. "Cool."

"Did you want me to add anything else? Make him do something crazy or *not* do something?" I offer genuinely, looking nearly straight up through his glasses into his deep blue eyes.

He smirks. "I think that'll be enough…for now." He chuckles. "Can I ask you one thing though?"

"Of course."

"Can you promise to never do that to me?" he says softly, holding my stare intently.

"I promise." I state every word emphatically because I mean it from the bottom of my heart.

"Thanks. I've got everything if you're ready to go…" He trails off.

Nodding, I turn on my heels and head back for the door. "Ready!"

Pulling into my manor, I can't help but stare at Greyson as his jaw unhinges and his eyes bulge out of his head.

"Vivian. This place is insane," he gasps, and I wish I could see it for the first time from his eyes.

Feeling his shock and admiration takes my breath away, and the closer we get to the front of the manor, the more intense those feelings become.

Circling around the ornate black fountain, I shift my car into park and speed around to his door, opening it for him. Am I usually this chivalrous? Not at all. But there's something about Greyson that makes me want to impress him. I like his smile, and the little things like this seem to earn that reaction.

"Vivian. There's no way this is your house. You actually live here?" he asks dumbfoundedly.

Nodding, I slide my arm into the crook of his elbow and guide him toward the long staircase leading to the gigantic black double doors. "I do. I've lived here for the last…few years."

"Few years?" He scoffs and pauses as we continue to ascend the stairs. "Do vampires really live forever? I guess I should ask you how old you are. Unless, of course, that's too intrusive."

"How old do you think I am?" I ask, curious about what he's thinking.

"I don't think that's a fair question." He laughs. "You look maybe twenty-one or twenty-two. But I know that can't be accurate. And if the rumors about vampires never aging are true, then you can really be any age and look the same."

"Not a bad assumption. And you are right. Although, I stopped aging at twenty-three. I just happen to have looked twenty-three for the last one hundred and forty years."

He halts and looks my way, studying my face as if he's searching for a mask, a way to reveal what I would really look like. But he won't find one.

Sensing his emotions, I prepare myself to feel disgust or repulsion. But I find neither. Instead, I find the same things I did the night we met—attraction and excitement.

"I have always had a thing for older women," he smirks, and I swear his eyes fucking shimmer in the light.

My stomach flutters, and I feel like a damn

teenager from my body's reaction to his light flirting. God, these next two weeks are going to be insatiable.

As we reach the top of the stairs, I unlock the black wooden door and pull it open. "Home sweet home."

"And I thought the outside was impressive," he murmurs breathlessly as we step inside the grand foyer.

"Well, I've had a few years to bring my vision to life." I stand still and watch him wander further into the open space, taking in every inch of my hard work.

A large chandelier hangs thirty feet in the air in the center of the foyer. The gold and white glowing lights are a stunning contrast to the heated dark hardwood floors. Every inch of this manor has been decorated with the utmost care by my very hand. This is my safe place, my sanctuary. One that I don't open up to others very often. But seeing his awe makes me think twice about that, wanting to show it off more in the future. The reds, pinks, creams, and black colors splashed all over the house bring it to life.

"This is beautiful, Vivian," he whispers, and my cheeks warm at his compliment.

It's like he's seeing a piece of myself that no one else does, and it feels strangely raw and vulnerable.

"Thank you," I say softly, moving to stand at his side.

He turns his head, looking down at me, and his focus bounces between my eyes.

He's so hot it's unnerving to stare at him for too long.

His strong bone structure but somehow soft demeanor is so alluring. Then there are those damn eyes that call my attention like a siren at sea, and I feel like if I look close enough, I can see the waves rolling in the depths of his gaze.

A loud meow pulls my focus away from Greyson, and I look toward the source, finding my pretty girl descending the stairs and trotting toward me.

"You have a cat?" he asks, immediately crouching and stretching out his hand.

"Oh, you should be careful. She doesn't like strangers…" I trail off as Lucy strides up to him and sniffs his fingers before leaning into his touch. "I guess you are an exception." *An exception to many things.*

He talks to her in a cute baby voice. "Aren't you sweet? What's your name?"

"Lucinda, or Lucy for short," I answer his question.

"Lucy is such a cute name," he coos to her.

The second she starts purring, I think I'm losing my mind because she has only ever purred for me, and definitely not for someone she just met. Although

I could count on one hand the number of people that have met her.

What is it with Greyson and the Barlowe girls? He makes us melt, I swear.

"How old is she?" he asks as Lucy's eyes drift close while her purrs fill the room.

"She's four years old. I found her as a kitten when she was two. Well, I guess she kind of found me. I came home one day, and she was sleeping on the front steps. We took to each other right away. Eventually, she followed me inside and never left." The memory of that day plays in my mind, and my heart warms.

She is the most important love of my life. I don't let myself get close to anyone anymore, not truly. I let people meet the surface version of Vivian, the parts I want the world to see, but other than Lucy, no one really knows what I'm like. And I prefer it that way.

Not even Ava and Skylar have been to my home. But it has nothing to do with them and everything to do with me. They are two of my closest friends. I've known them for years. We care deeply for one another, but we each have our secrets and respect each other's privacy.

"Will she live forever like you?" he asks genuinely.

Scoffing sadly, I sigh. "I wish. But unfortunately,

we don't have the capability of turning animals. If we did, I would have done it a long time ago."

He glances up at me with a tender gaze. "It's incredible that you will get to love countless animals in your long lifetime. You'll be able to make so many of their lives special and meaningful. She may not be yours forever, but you will always be hers."

My eyes well up, but I quickly blink them away, turning my gaze anywhere but his stare. "That's beautiful."

Walking toward the staircase, I change the subject. "We better get you settled into a room upstairs. Right this way."

"Do you sleep?" he asks, reminding me that he has a lot to learn about me and my kind as we begin to ascend the wide, ornate staircase.

Sliding my hand up the cold stone railing, I answer honestly, "We can if we choose to. But we don't need it to survive. It's more of an activity for us."

He follows closely behind me, and I can feel his stare on my body. "Interesting. Do you typically sleep?"

"Depends on the day. If Lucy curls up next to me and falls asleep, I'll usually sleep too. It makes me feel connected to her." As we reach the top of the stairs, I veer right and lead us toward my master suite.

"So, will I sleep with you?" He smiles at me, and I resist the urge to say something extra flirty.

Opening the door, I let him go in first. "You can sleep in here with me. Or there's spare bedrooms if you would prefer that."

"Why do you have so many extra bedrooms?" he asks, eyeing me curiously, a cocky smirk on his lips.

"I used to house newly turned vampires that needed help adjusting to their new world. They would practice their skills here. And practice mimicking humans so they could function in society. I still help some new vampires every now and then, but, umm…I don't really do it anymore. I like to keep my house to myself…" I trail off, not wanting to scare him before he's even settled in.

I can feel his curiosity pique, and I can tell he wants to know more. But thankfully, he doesn't push it further. We need to keep the boundaries where they are. He can explore the inside and outside of my body but he won't get my heart.

The thump of his bags makes me jump, and I hadn't realized I was so zoned into his stare and reading his emotions that I tuned everything else out.

The prettiest smile flashes on his face. "I'm going to stay in here…with you."

Good.

Swallowing hard, I suddenly feel nervous. I

haven't felt this out of control before, but I can't help it with him being so close to me. I want him to finish what we started earlier. But I also don't want to push him too far too soon.

"What are you thinking? Regretting your decision to bid for me?" he asks sweetly, and I glare at him as if that's the craziest thing he could have said.

"No. Of course not. I want you here," I murmur honestly, unsure of why I feel this way.

I swore off ever searching for romance again a long time ago. It's better if I'm alone; no one can be used as a pawn against me.

He steps forward, closing me in until the doorframe bumps into my back. "Oh really? You just want me for my blood, right? And maybe my talented fingers too." He waves them in the air in front of my face, and images of our fleeting moment flash in my mind.

His hand presses into the wall by my head as I nod, biting down on my bottom lip. "The only reasons, of course."

The thought of tasting his blood makes my entire body flutter with excitement, anticipation, and arousal. I've never craved someone's blood as much as I do his, and I have yet to even taste it.

I love our playful banter.

Rolling the sleeve of his long-sleeve T-shirt up, he

exposes the bulging veins of his forearms. "Drink up."

Fuck, I shouldn't find that as hot as I do.

"Are you sure you're ready?" I ask, pulling his arm up to my mouth.

He nods, and his breathing shallows out as he watches me with burning intensity. His nerves are skyrocketing, but beneath that slight twinge of fear lies unbounded excitement.

Opening wide, I pretend like I'm going to bite down, but I stop and pull away with bubbling laughter.

He furrows his brows.

"Firstly, I don't like drinking from the arm. It can be more painful for you because the veins are a lot smaller. Secondly, you're going to want to sit down."

His eyes widen slightly, and I feel a spike of worry from him. "It will hurt that bad?"

Shaking my head side to side, I push his chest gently until his legs hit the bed, and he drops down onto the comforter.

"I've been dying to get out of this dress," I mumble as I reach behind my back and tug the zipper down.

Pushing the thin straps off my shoulders, I shimmy it over my strapless bra, down my stomach, and past my lace panties until it pools at my feet.

His visceral reaction to my body makes me want to drop to my knees in front of him right now and make him feel as good as his fiery stare feels on me. I can feel his gaze tingling all across me, over every inch that he consumes.

Leaving my heels on, I step toward him and place my hand on his shoulder as I drop onto my knees on the bed, straddling him and lowering myself down into his lap.

"Is this what you'll wear every time you bite me? Because I think I could get used to it." His voice is raspy and low, tugging at my center.

Rolling my eyes playfully, I wrap my arms around his neck. "That could be arranged."

His hands fall to my hips, and the feeling of his fingers on my bare skin makes me feral. Every thought dissipates from my mind as I lean down and brush my lips against his. Once more. And then my restraint snaps.

Rolling my hips, I dip my tongue into his mouth simultaneously, and he grunts from my touch. Every movement makes me want more, and if it wasn't for his human fatigue, I would never stop.

He kisses me tenderly at first, but much like my own restraint, he loses his rather fast. Fisting his hand into my hair, he meets the roll of my hips with his own, his tongue claiming my mouth with every flick.

Shivers run through my body, and it takes everything in me to pull away.

Breathlessly, I whisper into his wet, parted lips, "I want to taste you so badly."

His hand drifts up my side until he grabs the bottom of my jaw. "Then bite me already."

Licking my bottom lip, I can feel my fangs wanting to protrude, but I resist them for a second more to say, "You can stop me at any time. It's not like the movies. I'm not a rabid animal. I'm in control of my thirst, not the other way around."

Nodding, he pulls me down to steal another kiss. "I understand."

His heartbeat is so loud in my ears, like a drum beating in my skull. "It will hurt right away, but it will fade quickly."

He kisses me again. "It's okay. I'm ready."

My fangs descend, and every sense heightens.

Sitting up taller, I gently tilt his head to the side. As if I'm looking through a microscope, I see his vein pulsing in his neck, and as if by their own accord, my fangs guide me directly to it.

I brush my thumb back and forth on Greyson's shoulder as I line my mouth up and sink my fangs deep into his neck.

The first few drops of his blood spill onto my tongue, and it's as if I'm feeding for the very first time, drinking liquid ecstasy. I want more, I *need* more.

Endorphins flood my body, and I can feel Greyson's doing the same.

We are vibrating together to our own frequency. The sound of our heartbeats is the drums, and the blood rushing through his veins is the melody, and I never want to stop listening.

Chapter Seven
greyson

She wasn't lying. It hurts like a fucking bitch when she bites into my neck. But it's gone as quickly as it appeared. And now, all I feel is… absolute euphoria.

Her tongue laps at my neck where her fangs are buried inside of me, and my dick twitches against her in response.

She was right. I've never felt anything like this. It's like my body is humming, floating above the ground, and she is the gravity keeping me rooted in place. I can feel her sucking the blood from my neck, and that alone is a new sensation altogether. Erotic and animalistic.

Snaking my arms around her waist, I roll my hips into her, and she moans, the vibrations coursing through my body, traveling through my veins. I repeat the motion again, and again, and again, until my mind is cloudy from the overwhelming pleasure.

I want my dick to be buried inside of her while her fangs are sunk into my neck. I want to fuck her senseless as she drinks from me. I want all of her. And I want it *right now*.

Fuck, I've never wanted something so badly in my life.

Every feeling and emotion is heightened, and it's…*intense*. Like the only thing in the world that matters right now is her. Maybe that's some weird vampire trick, or maybe that's just Vivian. I don't know, but I don't care.

Sliding my hands up her bare back, I grab the band of her bra and tug it gently before pausing, giving her a moment to grant me permission.

She nods, and her fangs shift, causing a twinge of stabbing pain to throb in their wake. I grunt, and her tongue massages the ache away. To be honest, I think I like the pain if it feels like *this* afterward.

Pinching the band of her bra, I undo the clasps and let it fall between us, revealing the two round breasts begging for my attention.

"Fucking hell, you are so sexy," I groan as I cup one in my hand, kneading it with my firm fingers.

She rocks her hips against me, and my cock twitches, begging to be set free. And it will be, soon enough.

Pinching her nipple, I roll it between my thumb and forefinger, feeling her back arch.

An odd sensation thrums in my neck, and a moment later, I feel her fangs release their hold on me, and she sits up in my lap, a stream of blood running down the side of her plump and swollen lips, rolling down her chin and neck.

Her hooded eyes are red, like they were when she first showed me what she was, and I still think they are really beautiful. Centered in her dark red stare are lust and desire-blown pupils.

"I figure for your first feeding, I shouldn't take too much. I don't want to tire you out too quickly." She hums, her lips reddened, a mix of lipstick and blood.

"Do I seem tired to you?" I groan, adjusting my hips as my rock-hard length grinds against her, begging to be set free.

She shakes her head with a naughty grin stretching across her face. She collects the running drops from her chin with her pointer finger and sucks it into her mouth, pulling it out with a popping sound.

"Well, how do I taste?" I ask her, my voice heavy and needy.

But she doesn't answer. She cups my face and crashes her lips to mine, kissing me ferally and desperately. And I eagerly match her pace.

Securing my hands on her back, I lift her up, spin around, and toss her onto the bed. Her eyes darken, and she wets her lips as she stares up at me hungrily.

Kneeling on the bed, I part her legs and glance down at her pretty cunt, veiled by thin black lace. "You got to taste me. It's only fair that I get to taste you."

"Make sure you get your fill, then. I want you to enjoy it," she hums, forcing her legs further apart as I lean forward, sliding my fingers beneath the lace and tugging them to the side.

"Fuck, you're already soaking wet," I growl, grabbing my length in my pants and adjusting myself so I don't burst through the seams.

I don't give her smart mouth a chance to respond. Lashing out, I plunge my tongue into her pussy, lapping her wetness up as I drag my tongue from her entrance up to her clit, sucking gently on the round bundle of nerves.

Her back arches as I bathe her with my kiss while sliding two fingers inside of her. I relentlessly lap and suck at her clit as she cries out into the room, filling it with helpless whimpers.

I want her to come like this, laid bare for me,

sprawled out on the bed with my blood drying on her neck. Hooking my fingers slightly, I pump them from knuckle to tip, faster and faster as her breathing quickens.

She starts tightening around me, and I know she's close. "Just like that baby, there you go." I flick my tongue against her clit, and she bucks her hips back and forth as I bring her to the edge, and just when she can barely take any more, I take her clit into my mouth, suckling on it while I finger fuck her.

She jumps off of the edge, her head falling back as she cries out while the orgasm tears through her.

I assume she'll need a second to gather herself, but in a blink, she's off the bed and standing behind me. As I turn around, she undoes my jeans and pulls them down along with my boxers.

My erection springs free, and she licks her lips again.

"I just *knew* you'd have a big dick," she murmurs as I slide off the bed and step out of my boxers.

Grabbing the back neck of my shirt, I pull it over my head, letting it drift down my arms and fall to the floor. "Is that some kind of vampire gift? Dick size detection?"

She chuckles and gently pushes me onto the bed. "No. That would be ridiculous. You just give off that energy."

"So you're happy with what you see, then?" I ask, sitting up on my elbows as she drops to her knees in front of the bed.

"Let me show you how much I love it." Her words are her only warning before she superspeeds her mouth to my dick and gently sucks the tip between her plump lips.

"Oh, *fuck*," I groan.

She takes more of me, working every inch into her mouth. When she has my entire length down her throat, her tongue flicks out, licking my balls, and I think I might keel over from the combined sensations. *Jesus, does she even have a gag reflex?*

"Holy shit, Vivian. That feels so fucking good," I growl as she lifts her head up, sliding me out of her mouth until only my tip remains.

As much as I don't want this to end, I need to be inside of her more than I need to breathe right now.

Running my hands along her jaw, I guide her up, claiming her lips with my own. "Let me fuck you, baby. Let me show you how perfect we fit together."

She nods against my kiss, and a second later, she effortlessly moves me up the bed like a rag doll, where I lie with my head on the pillows. I don't know if I'll ever be able to get used to her vampire speed.

She straddles my lap, running her soaking wet

center along my hardened length. I worry that feeling alone could send me over the edge.

"Do you have any condoms?" I ask her, wishing at this moment that I wouldn't be so responsible. "Can vampires even get pregnant?"

"We don't need them," she says before grinding her pussy against me again. "Besides, I want to feel every single vein of yours."

She lifts her hips, lining me up with her center, and slowly lowers herself onto me, my tip slipping inside of her, and I swear I see stars behind my eyelids.

"Oh fuck, you feel so good," I whimper while she takes more, gradually stretching herself around my cock.

"God, you're big, Greyson. Holy shit," she pants, resting her hands on my chest to steady herself.

When I twitch myself inside of her, she glares at me playfully, and I do little to hide my smile.

"Do it again," she murmurs, and I act on cue. "*Fuck.*"

Grabbing her lower waist, I move ever so slightly, and I feel her relax in my grip as she begins to ride me.

Her greedy little pussy grinds up my length before taking me back inside. Over and over, she uses my dick like her own personal toy.

"Oh shit, Greyson," she cries out, and I'm thankful she's not going to last much longer because neither am I at this moment.

Gripping her hips tighter, I stop her movement and hold her in place as I thrust upward, burying myself to the hilt with each motion.

She moans and whimpers as I bring us each to the edge of oblivion. And as she tightens around me, we come hard together, waves of pleasure pulsing through our bodies.

We stay there for what feels like minutes, the sounds of our breathing—more so mine as she is magically not out of breath—the only sounds in the room. Her stamina must be amazing.

"Vivian, that...*you*...holy fuck." My incoherent thoughts leave me, and the most beautiful, bashful smile takes over her face, lighting it up.

"Best feeding *ever*," she murmurs, pursing her lips.

She slides off me and grabs a towel from the bathroom as I ask, "Do you not normally have sex with the human you're drinking from?"

She eyes me curiously as she delicately cleans me up. "A very long time ago when I was younger, yes. It's happened once or twice. But it's never felt like...*that*."

I blink and she's gone, but I hear her words cut

through the empty room like a ghost's whisper. "I'm going to change quickly. Be right out."

I'm never going to get used to that super-speed thing or the fact that she can move me with ease, like when she slid me up the bed. It was…oddly attractive. But I doubt there is anything about her that I wouldn't like.

"Jesus Christ!" I shout as she suddenly appears in the empty space beside me.

Bubbling laughter leaves her pretty lips. Grabbing a pillow from behind me, I lightly hit her with her, which does little to calm her giggle fit.

Stretching my arms out, I sit up and walk over to my bag, grabbing a fresh pair of boxers to sleep in and slip them on before climbing back into bed beside her.

She's now cuddling the pillow I hit her with like a stuffed animal.

A thought drifts into my mind. "Do you dream?"

She nods and looks up at me through her long lashes. "We can, but it's rare unless we take a drug to help induce it."

"Are there special vampire drugs? Or do you just do a bump of coke?" I laugh.

She side-eyes me humorously. "No, we don't do coke—well, at least I don't. I doubt it would have any effect on vampires; most human drugs don't. There's an apothecary in town that we can get it from. The paranormal drugs wouldn't do anything if they were ingested by a human. It affects us differently. A lot of things do."

"I want to know *everything*," I mumble, resting my head on the pillow next to hers.

She nestles closer to me. "You will. But first, you need to get some sleep."

In a matter of hours, everything about my life has changed. She has me for the next two weeks. But then what? What happens when I leave this mansion?

How am I ever going to go back to my normal life after this?

Chapter Eight
vivian

The second Greyson woke up, he couldn't stop asking a thousand questions, so I figured we could go on a field trip today. Which is why we are heading to Ashwood Apothecary right now, run by my favorite witch, Autumn Ashwood, and her family.

Meeting him outside, I pull Greyson to the side to give him a little backstory before we head in, as I spent the last five minutes during our drive answering his questions about what it's like to feed on someone and didn't have a chance to tell him.

I start with a question that has an obvious answer. "You know what I am, right?"

He stares at me with a mischievous gleam in his eyes. "I sure hope so after last night."

My cheeks burn as the memories of last night flash in my mind. "It's not just vampires and humans that inhabit this world."

His eyes practically bulge out of his head, and I swear I can see the wheels turning behind those gorgeous blue orbs. "Are you serious?"

"Very," I murmur. "You are about to meet some. Autumn, she and her family run this shop."

He looks around as if a witch is just going to jump out at him before leaning forward, his hand nonchalantly falling to my waist as he whispers, "What are they?"

Glancing up, I lose my train of thought for a moment because he looks so angelic in the sunlight.

The bright rays make his hair seem like it's glowing. His features are carefully caressed by the light, highlighting the sharpness of his cheekbones and jawline yet the softness of his eyes and welcoming part of his lips.

The bell of a shop a few feet from us chimes, pulling me out of my stupor, and I clear my throat. "Ashwood Apothecary is owned by witches."

"Like real-life ride-on-a-broom witches?" he gasps.

Rolling my eyes, I scoff. "No, they don't ride on

brooms. I mean, they used to, for sure, but that is something of the past. It was a gift that passed through different bloodlines of witches. I'm not even sure it still exists anymore."

"Goddamn," Greyson mumbles breathlessly.

"What?"

"You have made my life so much more interesting." He pauses, holding my stare and looking deeply into my eyes. "What am I supposed to do after this? Pretend I don't know that witches run this shop when I pass by? It's going to be impossible."

"I could always make you forget," I smirk maliciously, tapping on the side of his head.

He squints his eyes playfully. "You wouldn't."

Shrugging, I hook my arm in his and lead us down the walkway toward Ashwood's. "There could be others shopping here."

"Witches?" he murmurs.

"Yeah. But also other vampires, and maybe even humans."

As another question begins to roll off his tongue, I grab the door and pull it open, gesturing him inside. "I'll tell you more later. Come on."

"You better, or I'm cutting you off," he whispers into my ear, and I can't help the smile that forms on my lips.

Greyson walks past me, stepping into the

apothecary, his eyes immediately scanning every inch of the main room. Crystals decorate the large table in the center of the area, from palm stones and tumbled to centerpieces and massive specimens.

But my gaze drifts to Autumn, where she stands behind the checkout counter, helping a customer who is radiating excitement.

Autumn's parents named her perfectly, an embodiment of the magical season itself. Her hair flows down her shoulders in loose waves, the shade of a pretty orange leaf in the heart of fall.

She smiles at the customer she's with, the freckles on her nose and her gorgeous green eyes scrunching up. I let Greyson wander while I make my way over to her.

"Have a great day, Maria!" Autumn chimes as she hands over the purchases in a recyclable bag with the apothecary's logo stamped onto the side.

"You too," Maria sings before spinning on her heels and striding past me with joy.

"Vivian, you look radiant as always," Autumn compliments me as I rest my hands atop the counter.

"You are always generous with your praise. You look incredible yourself."

"Why, thank you," she boasts, giving me a little twirl, the skirt of her mocha-colored dress billowing out. "What are you in for today? And..." She lowers her voice. "Is *he* with you?"

Nodding, I grin. "He is. I'm giving him a little introduction to our world while he stays with me, and I thought you would be the perfect place to start. Besides, I need to pick up more cookies for Lucy—she's almost out. And she gets grumpy if she doesn't have her favorite treats at the ready."

Autumn's lips part, revealing that perfect white smile. "She is my favorite customer. I'll go get a bag ready for her."

The plus side of having a witch as a friend is, well...having a witch as a friend. It's quite self-explanatory, really.

But Lucy's personal benefit is that she gets to eat cookies that lengthen her lifetime so that she gets to stay with me for a couple additional years. It won't make her live forever, but every bonus day counts.

Plus, the cookies are Lucy's favorite snack, and she would eat the entire stash all at once if I let her. They may enhance her youth, but it still won't protect her from tummy aches. Besides, the spell only works once a day. If she were to eat all of the cookies, it wouldn't have any different effect than if she only ate one.

The cookies are spelled by Autumn, a secret and a formula that only she knows. She placed this safeguard on it so that the cookies couldn't be abused to achieve immortality. That's not their purpose. And messing around with immortality is a dangerous game to play with. Magic has limitations to what it will allow before demanding great prices.

Autumn's flowy dress sways side to side as she walks toward the back rooms to get my order.

"Find anything you like?" I ask Greyson, turning to find him carefully studying the display case of ingredients.

"What could you possibly need feathers of a raven for?" he chuckles, pointing at the massive jar of black feathers.

With no one else in the store, I answer truthfully, not masking the truth for human ears. "Me personally? Nothing. But witches often use them in potions or spell enhancers. And humans typically buy them as a fun gag gift or knickknack for their own collection."

"Interesting..." He trails off, meandering from the wall of glass jars to a display of DIY potion kits. "Are these real?"

"To a human with no magic? The potions won't do anything special. But for a witch, it's an easy kit to grab and go for whatever they need."

"Hmm. Smart marketing," he mumbles, fascinated by it, and I can't help but chuckle.

"Do you want a potion kit? I'll buy you one. My treat," I offer playfully.

He flashes a glare at me. "Only if it comes with magic. Otherwise, no, thank you."

"Which one would you get?" I ask him out of curiosity.

He taps his finger on his chin as he studies the kits before grabbing one and holding it up. "This one."

"A love potion? Really? Are you worried your own charm won't be enough for a girl?"

He holds my stare firmly, not an eyelash moving from place. "Is it enough for you?"

Shit.

I don't know why that caught me so off guard, but the warmth building deep inside my chest nearly brings tears to my eyes. I don't know how he's managing to hop over every barrier I have built, but it's unnerving how much I don't seem to mind.

I wasn't entirely sure I could still have that reaction with someone. I buried those parts of myself away so deeply that they could never be found again. And I don't know whether I want to hold on to it or run far away.

My cheeks warm of their own will nonetheless, and thankfully, Autumn saves me from having to come up with something to say, "Here you go. Two scoops for the best girl."

"Are you referring to Lucy or me?" I grin.

"Lucy, *duh*," she says straight-faced before she hands over the brown sack bag and a black box. "Here's the council's order for antidote potions by the way. I was going to call you this morning, but you saved me the trouble."

"Oh perfect. Thank you."

Antidote potions are used to counteract vampire venom. But they require one more ingredient before activating—the blood of the vampire who bit them. Without it, they are pretty jars full of witchy ingredients. A decoration is all they'd be good for.

We keep a large stock of them at the Barlowe, and I keep my own stock at the house. You never know when you're going to need it.

Turning, I call out to Greyson, "Are you getting anything?"

He shakes his head as he strides over to me, his hands tucked in his jean pockets, not stopping until his leg is brushing against the pantyhose on my upper thigh. "No, thank you. I wouldn't even know where to begin."

"I love your skirt, by the way, Vivian," Autumn compliments me.

Rising onto the balls of my feet and back down, I study my outfit. Black turtleneck tucked into a tight black-and-white plaid tulip skirt with black pantyhose beneath and cute black combat-style boots.

"Thanks," I murmur politely and hand her cash to cover my bill plus tip, which she carefully stows in the register.

"I'm Autumn," she greets Greyson, sticking her hand over the counter. "It is so nice to meet you. Autumn's never brought one of her bloodlings here before."

It's no secret to Autumn that Greyson is my bloodling. I don't keep humans in my company, except for during the Culling, although typically I spend mere minutes with them, and I never parade them around in public.

But at this point, the entire vampire community knows about my participation in the Culling. If they weren't at the event, I'm sure the gossip would have already traveled to them and fast.

"Is that so?" he asks, side-eyeing me while sticking his hand out to her.

The second her hand connects with his, she sucks in a sharp breath, her eyes widening and face paling. Goose bumps erupt on my arms at her reaction.

If it were anyone else, I wouldn't have thought twice, but despite Autumn's petite size, her power is immaculately strong.

Opening my senses up to her, I am knocked back by the intense surprise, confusion, and worry.

"What?" I bite out, demanding to know what she's thinking.

She studies him quizzically. "I don't know." She pauses like she's trying to decipher what just happened. "I felt your energy intertwined with his. I've never experienced that before. It was…very odd."

Well, what the fuck does that mean?

"It's probably just me having an off day. It happens all of the time, more than I would like to admit." She laughs painfully, but I don't miss the forcefulness of her breath or the denial emanating from her that she couldn't hide if she tried.

Holding her stare, I give her a look that I know she'll understand. One that says, *We'll discuss this later.*

She nods before planting a smile on her lips. "I'm sure I will see you both again soon."

"Bye, Autumn!" Looping my arm in Greyson's, I lead us out of the door.

Greyson clears his throat. "Was that weird to you? Or just weird to me? Although, right now, everything is weird to me."

I chuckle. "Probably just you. Autumn is always like that though—she can't help it. Her magic is strong, and sometimes it can be uncontrollable. I'm sure that's what happened back there. She was probably just confusing our energies."

"Our energies?" he asks, and I realize I should probably explain myself.

"Witches can sense people's energy either by touch or scent. It depends on the witch and their bloodline. It's how they know who is who at their core and *what* they are. Every individual has their own energy wave. Like how humans tell others apart from their fingerprints and DNA, witches do so with energy. Like she said, she has off days. I'm sure that's why she thought she sensed my energy on you."

"Could it have just rubbed off? Like from last night?" he asks as we near my car.

Shrugging, I brush off his concern. "Yeah, probably. I don't know exactly how it works."

He seems to accept my answer, and I don't say another word about it.

But that couldn't be further from the truth. I know all about witches and their energy readings. What I don't understand is why my energy was recognizable in him. I need to see her again without Greyson. She held back, not wanting to scare him, but I need the truth because Autumn knew that sensing my energy in him should be impossible, but she lied.

And so did I.

Chapter Nine
greyson

Waking up this morning with Vivian in my arms is something I never knew I needed or even wanted.

Somehow, last night was even better than the first time, and I honestly don't know how that's even fucking possible. I don't know if it has something to do with the feeding or if it's just her, but I think I might be addicted.

I still can't get over how crazy this is yet so natural. There is something sexy about the fact that my very blood is keeping her alive. It's…invigorating. I want her to drink from me constantly. I love knowing it's my blood that's pumping through her veins when I bury myself inside of her.

She's insatiable. Beautiful. Mysterious. I want to know everything about her.

Glancing at the clock on the nightstand, I shift my arms tighter around her. It's only six thirty, but knowing that she's right here makes me not want to go back to sleep. For the first time, the reality is better than the dream.

Am I reading too much into this? Am I romanticizing everything that's happened so far? Is it bad that I don't care if I have been?

All I know is that my entire life, I have been searching for a greater purpose. I knew in the pit of my stomach that there was something bigger waiting for me. I survived the early years of my life, then spent the following decade yearning for consistency and comfort.

I reached the stability I was after, and I convinced myself that it was enough. I chose a realistic career path, one that would guarantee high salaries. My extracurriculars didn't involve heavy drinking or drugs. I made smart decisions. I did everything right…*right?*

But now, looking back, I can't pinpoint a single time where I chose something because I wanted to.

Carefully, I crafted my future with logistics instead of passion.

Where has it gotten me? I'm months away from graduating with a degree that I don't really even want to use. I'm not passionate about finance; I'm simply good at it.

I keep to myself because the fewer moving factors, the more predictable an outcome. I have no friends, a roommate I despise, a future I'm not sure I even want, and a life that is about to change with the money I'm getting from Vivian.

For the first time, I feel like I have the freedom to chase what I want because I already have what I need. After this arrangement is over, I won't need to pursue a job simply because of financial reasons.

I've spent my life reading stories to fill the void of excitement and adventure. I read to discover more in this world. But I never knew that I would stumble into the making of a story of my own.

Even though I know what Vivian and I have will come to an end, for the time being, I want to pretend there's a chance it might not. No matter how much it may hurt afterward, I would rather open myself up to her, be raw and vulnerable, and enjoy her time while she gives it to me before it runs out.

"You're awake," she states rather than asks, her

voice as smooth as silk, drawing me away from my rambling thoughts.

Nodding, I nestle my head into the crook of her neck, trailing kisses from the base to her ear. "How'd you know?"

She softly melts in my embrace. "Your heart rate spiked, and your breathing became uneven."

"Hmm. Sounds like you made that up," I tease her, knowing damn well that she is telling the truth.

My arm falls, bouncing off the mattress. She's gone. Instead of snuggled in bed with me, she's across the room, leaning against the dresser with a devilish smirk on her lips.

Her arms are crossed over my T-shirt that she wore to bed, completely oversized on her body, stopping just on the tops of her thighs.

Rolling over onto my back, I stretch my arms up and tuck them beneath my head, my elbows jutting out to the sides.

A cool breeze skates across my abs. "You look better in my shirts than I do."

"Yeah?" she murmurs, playing with the bottom hem.

Running my stare from her painted toes up her long legs, I study her more intensely than anything before, trailing high, and right as I'm about to lock with her gaze, I suck in a breath.

Perhaps it's because I'm starting to get used to this little trick of hers, but I know my gaze won't fall on her. Because she's already moved or teleported. I laugh to myself.

"Ugh," I grunt with surprise as she lands on top of me, straddling my waist and planting her hands lightly on my chest. My hands fall to her hips. "Do you want to start your day with a sip from your new favorite drink?"

She chuckles softly. "You just woke up. I thought I would give your human body a moment to adjust."

Digging my fingers into her bare hips, I grind upward into her center. "Oh, don't worry. I'm adjusting just fine."

A red flush flickers across her cheeks, and a coy smile lifts her lips. But as her eyes fall to mine, I can't help but notice a swirling darkness dance deep in her gaze, one that only someone else who's experienced the true pains of life can recognize.

Lifting my hand up, I tap the side of her head. "What's happening in there?"

Whether she doesn't want to talk about it or just doesn't want to tell me, she dismisses my concern with a wave. "What? Nothing."

It's not my place to push the topic, so I let it go. At least for now.

She changes the subject with a smile. "I deposited

the first part of your funds into your account this morning."

"Thank you," I tell her honestly. She has no idea what this means to me. She is single-handedly changing my entire life.

"Ask me something," she murmurs softly, trailing her hands down my sternum and abs.

A thousand questions begin popping up in my mind.

What is it like being able to move that fast?

What's it like to have all of the money in the world and want for nothing?

What other beings are out there?

What was your childhood like?

Why, after all of this time, do you still live alone?

Are vampires doomed to isolation?

The questions are almost overwhelming, but I eventually decide on one.

Reaching up and stroking her cheek, I ask, "You asked me what I want out of this. But what do *you* want? Besides the obvious."

Her eyes soften, her brows furrowing ever so slightly as her lips part. But nothing comes out.

"Is that too invasive?" I ask, wondering if I overstepped.

"No, not at all." She forces a smile. "I want

exactly what we've already been doing. Feeding. Fucking. What's another good f-word?"

"Frolicking?" I offer, earning a smile.

"Feeding. Fucking. Frolicking…where to exactly?" she asks with humor dancing beneath her words.

"Anywhere you want to go." I pause. "Is this where I ask you if that's all you want? The same way you asked me."

Her eyes fog over as if a memory is playing out before them. "I want you to enjoy yourself. That's what I want. To drink from you while making you feel things no one ever has. Your pleasure is mine too. *Literally*." Her delicate fingers brush the skin of my side, her thumb swiping back and forth. Her eyes brighten like a lightbulb goes off in her head. "I don't think I've told you the other little gift I have."

"What do you mean?"

"Do you know how I told you about witches being able to sense energy?"

I nod.

"Well, I can sense and feel other people's emotions. Anger. Happiness. If they're being deceitful or honest." Her voice softens. "If they're turned on."

"Hmm. Since the night we met you've been able to feel exactly what you do to me?" I ask, biting down on my bottom lip.

She shrugs, smirking. "Yeah. I have

"And you know what I'm feeling right now?" I murmur, my heart racing as I fidget with the hem of her t-shirt.

Smiling, she nods slowly.

Every second of every day, she ceases to amaze me.

She swallows hard before continuing with our original conversation, her gaze falling to my chest. "I want you to leave our arrangement with the capability of doing whatever you want with your life. Which is why I'm tripling the funds you were initially told you'd receive."

My body stiffens. "What? Vivian, no. You're already giving me plenty."

Her playfulness returns as she smirks and says, "Try to stop me. You won't be able to. I'm much faster than you."

She told me that I would be receiving three hundred thousand, but now she's giving me nearly a million dollars. It's almost impossible to comprehend that amount of money.

"It's too much," I insist.

She giggles. "Trust me, it's not. Greyson, I want you to have the life you desire. This money won't dent my account, so please stop fighting me on it. You are the most genuine and honest person I've ever met. I want you to have it."

I know if I open my mouth to say anything else, I'll protest her generosity. So instead, I show her my thanks in another way.

Skating my hands up her sides, I grab her face and pull her down to me, capturing her mouth with mine.

Licking the seam of her lips, I taste the inside of her mouth as my fingers find the hem of the shirt she's wearing and bunch it up right above her hips.

We devour each other with our kisses, our tongues melting together. Her lips are silky soft as they melt against mine, only parting long enough to gasp for air. But I'm willing to suffocate as long as she doesn't stop kissing me.

I pull away just enough to whisper, "What was it you said you wanted? Feeding and fucking?"

Grabbing the cotton fabric, I lift it up over her bare breasts, which bounce from the motion, making my mouth water as I lift the shirt over her head and drop it to the floor.

Tipping my head to the side, I tap my neck with two fingers. "I'm all yours."

She wets her lips, her hazel gaze turns dark red, and two white fangs protrude as she bites down on her bottom lip. In the blink of an eye, I feel her sink into my neck, pain and pleasure blending into eternal ecstasy.

Vivian took me on a private tour of Saint Eldritch yesterday, showing me places I've somehow never been. Or maybe it felt that way because I'm looking at everything through a new lens.

She also told me some things I was desperate to know. I learned that vampires don't eat human food. They can consume it just fine, but their body discards it, disintegrating it the second it hits their stomach. That might be the sole reason I would change into a vampire. Bottomless calories for life.

Many of the things I thought I knew about vampires prior to meeting Vivian turned out to be false. They have a reflection in the mirror. Garlic does absolutely nothing to them. Same goes for crosses. They don't need to breathe air to survive. They can't suffocate. Their bodies just held on to that involuntary movement after death as a tool to help them trick their victims into thinking they're human.

But a few traits about her kind turned out to be true. They live for eternity. They survive on human blood. And a stake through the heart is deadly, but only when it's carved from a white ash tree.

She patiently sat and answered a thousand questions for me before she had to leave to attend to some High Council business, leaving Lucy and me home alone.

Vivian said that Lucy doesn't like new people, but that doesn't apply to me because she's started to follow me everywhere I go in the house, including the bathroom. She has lost all regard for privacy.

It's been a few days since I got a good run in, so when I woke up this morning, I changed into joggers and a hoodie, slipped on my tennis shoes, secured my phone in my chest bag, and headed out for a run.

It takes me about five minutes to even get off Vivian's property and get back into the community. I've never been on this side of town, and I quickly understand why. Every house I pass looks like it was plucked out of a magazine. Not a single one of these houses looks like it's less than ten million dollars. Every driveway has a private security gate. The landscaping consists of trimmed hedges and perfectly maintained flower beds, although with the weather cooling down, a majority of them are starting to fade.

Deciding that I need to see parts of this town I feel like I belong in, I travel the mile toward the center of town, near the apothecary we visited. Music plays in my ears, drowning out the noise of the cars driving by and the rest of the world.

As I turn onto a new street, a small pit forms in

my stomach like a warning sign. Coming to a halt, I decide that today is not the day to investigate that feeling.

Spinning around, I dig my feet into the ground and take off, following the same path back toward Vivian's. But I still can't shake that feeling…the sense that someone is watching me. Goose bumps erupt on my arms, but I chalk it up to the brisk fall air.

The hair on my neck rises as I cross back into the wealthy, ritzy neighborhood, and I tap my earbud to stop the music. I want to be able to hear around me.

Turning my head, I glance back behind me, but I don't see anyone. This is weird. I'm probably overanalyzing it. Creating it all in my head. The idea that I sense someone watching me is manifesting into a real sensation like a paranormal hypochondriac.

Running down the main road, I turn right at the end to head up the short hill to Vivian's place. But even as I try to force the thoughts of someone following me out of my mind, I fail.

As I turn into her long, winding driveway, lined by tall pine trees, the hair on the back of my neck settles back down, and the eeriness looming over me dissipates. I don't know if I should tell Vivian or not. I don't want to freak her out if there's nothing to freak out over. Besides, if someone was watching me, it could have been innocent. I just can't help the tingle in the back of my brain that knows that wasn't the case.

Jogging up the front steps, I pull my sweatshirt off over my head, wiping the pouring sweat from my face and letting the wind cool down my body. Crossing my fingers on top of my head, I take a few deep breaths to calm my erratic breathing and racing heart. As I take one last deep breath through my nose, I open the front door and step inside, immediately hearing someone rustling around in the kitchen.

"Hello?" I call out, shutting the door, slinging my hoodie over my shoulder, and walking across the giant space toward the open kitchen.

No one responds.

Lucy jumps down from the couch and runs over the second she sees me, and I bend down to give her soft head a few pets, earning sweet purrs.

A pot clatters to the floor in the kitchen, and I rush over, the culprit finally coming into view as I turn the corner and find Vivian viciously mixing something in a bowl.

She freezes the second she sees me, her eyes softening.

"What's going on in here?" I ask, examining the endless ingredients strewn across the island.

She huffs, humor gleaming in her eyes as she

returns her focus to the bowl. "I'm making breakfast."

My heart clenches as I take a seat on a stool on the opposite side of the island. "You don't eat food."

Her gaze flicks up to me from the bowl, glaring at me through her dark, long eyelashes. Her lips part, but before she says a word, she hesitates and takes a deep breath. "I'm making them for you."

Tingles dance across my chest at her words. "You're making *me* breakfast?"

"Oh no, you don't have an allergy or anything, do you? Do you even eat muffins? Shit, I totally didn't ask," she apologizes, and I reach my hand across the island and rest it on top of hers.

"First, take a breath for me. I don't have any allergies. And I love muffins." I smile, my throat burning as I debate whether or not to share more.

"What is it, then?" she asks, her eyes searching mine.

"What do you mean?"

She calmly sets the bowl and whisk down. "I could feel your discomfort."

Honest to God, I have no idea how I forgot about that special talent of hers.

Closing my eyes, I smile softly before meeting her concerned stare. "That has absolutely nothing to do with you."

A moment of silence passes between us.

Mustering up the nerve to open up, I clear my throat. "It means a lot that you're doing this." I pause, wondering where to even start. "I didn't have a lot of home-cooked meals growing up. I bounced around a lot between foster homes. A lot of them didn't provide or care the way they should've."

She listens intently, flipping her hand over and caressing mine as I continue. "I got lucky at the end though, ending up in the care of Cheryl Harper. She was the first person who ever really cared about where I ended up. She was my family and the best person I've ever known. I wish I had told her that more before she passed. Other than her, I've never really had someone make me breakfast before."

A blade rakes down my throat as I finish, the vulnerability making me nauseous.

"I'm sorry life wasn't kinder to you. You deserved better than that. But I'm glad that you had her," she murmurs, her voice soft and warm. "How long ago did she pass?"

"A few years now. She went out doing one of her favorite things—napping." I chuckle, reminiscing at her love for afternoon snoozes.

She grins. "Sounds like a good way to go."

"Yeah," I mumble.

She glances down at the bowl. Her nostrils flare

and eyebrows pinch as a tear wets her lashes. "I got this recipe from a friend of mine. She used to make these all the time, and I remember how delicious they were. I could never quite get them to turn out the same as her though. Hers were always better."

I know the look in her eyes, recognizing the fogginess that forms when you recall a memory of someone who's no longer with you. Sliding my hand from hers, I rise from my stool and walk around the island, leaning my back against the counter, my fingers wrapped under the lip.

She turns around and leans next to me, her arm resting against mine.

"What was her name?"

She smiles hauntingly as she looks down at the hardwood floor. "Genevieve." She gulps hard. "God, it's been so long since I spoke her name out loud. She was sunshine personified. Her hair was light like yours, but her eyes were almost identical to mine. She was so beautiful and kind."

My heart aches for her. I don't need her ability to be able to tell how painful this is for her to recall.

"I'm sorry," I whisper, dropping my hand and intertwining my fingers with hers.

She tilts her head up, her hazel stare peering up at me through the pool of tears gathering in her eyes. "It's okay. It's nice, actually. To talk about her."

"It's the way we keep the ones we lost alive."

A gleam of hope sparkles in her eyes. "Yeah. You're right."

Turning to face her, I lift my hand and swipe the tears away from her eyes, stroking her cheeks. "You can tell me about her anytime you'd like. I'd love to hear some stories."

She nods sharply. "I have so many good ones." She sighs. "She was my best friend in the whole wide world. But she was human. At the time, I hadn't realized how much my position on the council put a target on the back of the ones I loved. Until it was too late…" Her voice cracks. "Vampires who don't follow the rules of the council and respect humans are referred to as rogues. Well, one decided that he was tired of the council trying to control him.

Her gaze drops to my chest as she continues to open up. "He couldn't hurt me if he tried. I've been around long enough to learn how to protect myself. But Genevieve didn't. One night, we were supposed to meet up after she got off of work at the bakery. But then she didn't show, which was extremely out of character for her. She didn't answer her texts or calls, so I went looking for her." She sucks in a shuddering breath. "When I got to the bakery, I found her, and she was gone. Someone drained her completely. The worst part is that I was going to turn her that night…she was supposed to be with me forever."

My chest burns for her, and I wish I could help ease the pain. For the first time, I see her walls crumble down. And fuck, the pain that's laced in her pretty hazel orbs is enough to stab me in the heart a million times over.

When you lose someone that close to you, you lose pieces of yourself too, leaving tiny holes in your heart that ache for what's been lost.

"I know she's not here by your side. But in a way, she will live forever because of you and your love for her."

Her cheeks still cupped in my hands, she nods her head slowly. Holding my stare, she rises onto the tips of her toes and slides a hand along my jaw. Her forehead rolls against mine as her heavy breathing finally begins to slow.

"Thank you," she whispers against my lips before gently pressing hers into me, kissing me tenderly and slowly as my heart begins to rattle in its cage, the bars loosening.

Chapter Ten
vivian

I'm utterly screwed, irrevocably ruined by Greyson.

Since I've met him, I've started breaking every boundary and rule I set for myself without much of a thought.

I went too far, I opened up too much and let him in more than he ever should have been, and I truly don't know if I'm going to be able to let Greyson walk away when our time is up. It's going to be damn near impossible.

Needing fresh air and a brief second away from him to clear my mind, I decide to run a few errands this morning before he wakes.

Forcing the thoughts of him from my mind, I focus on the task at hand. I'm going to pick up some food from a list of favorites that were on Greyson's info card from the Culling.

I could have had one of the High Council's assistants do it for me, but I needed to step off cloud nine for a moment just to reflect. We've been living in our own bubble for a few days now, and I can't even think straight.

My first stop this morning is Ashwood Apothecary. Although I've been blissfully enjoying the past few days, I still cannot get the interaction between Autumn and Greyson out of my mind. It was bizarre, to say the least. And it's been weighing on me.

Even though I don't have Greyson tagging along, I still choose to drive because I don't mind if my errands take a little longer.

Parking in front of the apothecary, I slide out of the car and take a deep breath of the crisp fall air, notes of fresh apples and cinnamon invading my nose. This is the best time of year. Not too hot, not too cold. The leaves transform into the most beautiful shades of red, orange, and yellow.

But none are more beautiful than the large oak tree that grows behind the apothecary. The leaves are some of the last to fall, but they turn a breathtaking deep reddish-purple. I've made it a part of my routine to swing by and see it at least a handful of times before the branches are completely bare each year.

The air changes from cool to a welcoming warmth as I step inside of the shop, quickly greeted by Autumn. "Good morning, Vivian!"

"Hi, Autumn. How's it going?" I ask her politely as a shiver races down my spine from the temperature change.

The Ashwoods and I have had a relatively close relationship for years. Unfortunately, the story of Autumn and I meeting is a rather sad one. I saved her from a few rogue vampires that tried attacking her a few years back. Although, perhaps "tried" isn't the right word because they succeeded to some degree.

Thankfully, I had arrived before they were able to kill her. But that doesn't mean that they didn't harm her in other ways. They certainly did, and I made them pay for it dearly—torturing them for hours before giving them the mercy of death.

Rogue vampires refuse to abide by the rules of the High Council, abusing and using humans like hospital blood bags. They have no respect for them or the rest of us. But they've practically been extinct for years. We haven't heard of any movement of one for almost a decade.

Autumn's parents were grateful to me for saving

their daughter, allowing me to shop for free anytime in their store. But I've never taken them up on their offer. I have enough money to never worry, and they have a small business I love to support.

Autumn's smile is beaming like always as she responds, "Great. We just got some new crystal jewelry if you'd be interested in it at all."

Her offer piques my interest, but I remind myself why I'm here. "Maybe another day. But first, we need to talk."

A knowing look flashes in her eyes. She knows exactly what I'm here for. "I figured you would be back for that."

"Care to explain what you *really* felt that day?" I ask her for the truth, knowing she only concealed it because of Greyson's presence.

She sighs. "Honestly, Vivian, I have no idea what happened. It's never been like that before. I shouldn't have sensed any of your energy in him. It was like your and his energy were wound together as one."

Well, I was really hoping she would have an easy explanation. But of course it wouldn't be simple when it comes to Greyson. To be honest, it's been weird from the start.

"What does that mean, then?" I ask her, walking over the counter she's resting against, trailing my finger along the marble top.

"I can ask around, see if anyone's heard of it or something like it," she offers, and I open myself up to her senses, biting my tongue hard when all I feel from her is concern.

"What is your gut telling you?" I ask her. "Your instinct is powerful, Autumn. Don't shy away from it."

She hesitates, holding my stare intently before taking a deep breath. "You're connected to him somehow, in a way I don't understand. But I can't help but feel wary of it. Whatever it is, I can sense power lurking beneath the surface." She holds my stare before chuckling. "I probably sound insane."

Still tapped into her emotions, I sense the genuineness in her words and the lie in her dismissal.

My chest is winding up, my breaths getting stuck in the twists and turns. "I don't think you ever sound insane."

This entire arrangement is dangerous enough for Greyson, let alone whatever the hell is happening now. I bought him in the auction because I was selfish and couldn't stand the thought of another vamp's fangs in him. Now, all I've done is leave my mark on him in some unknown way.

Is that my curse? Getting the humans I like killed?

I'm torn between telling her about the first time Greyson and I met and keeping it a secret for a while longer. I didn't think too much of it at the time. But the fact that his words demanded to be noticed by me without effort should have been impossible. I've never had that happen before. He overrode the walls I keep up.

"Do you know something else that you're not telling me?" Autumn murmurs, pulling me from the internal debate as she eyes me cautiously.

Opening my senses further, I don't feel anyone else in the vicinity. We're alone. "Maybe. I don't know if it would even be helpful."

She matches my secretive tone. "More information can't hurt anything."

"It's hard to explain." I pause, trying to think of something she could relate to, and it dawns on me. "I imagine when you sense energies, you open yourself up to it. Like a window. Would you say that's correct?"

She nods. "Yeah, like opening a part of myself to allow the energy to flow through me."

"The same goes for me with reading emotions and tapping into my hyper-hearing. Ever since I've learned how to control it, I have to engage that sense inside of me for it to work." I pause, taking a slow, steady breath. "Except for the night I met Greyson."

She listens to me intently, her green gaze boring into me as I continue. "Some friends and I went to a club in town, and almost immediately after I entered the place, I heard his voice so clearly, as if he were standing right next to me."

"Okay?" she questions softly.

"My hyper-hearing wasn't engaged, and he was nowhere in sight. His voice invaded me, and I had no choice but to listen."

The wheels begin turning behind her gaze. "Only his?"

"Yes."

Her brows furrow. "Initially, I assumed that the connection would have begun after you started feeding, but at that point, you had never bitten him, right?"

"No, I didn't even know him."

She jots down a few notes. "Was there anything else weird? The smallest details could help."

"Aside from me thinking he's insanely hot? No. But he's attractive as hell, so I can't fathom that's a paranormal thing, more so a Vivian and Greyson thing." I chuckle.

She grins at my laugh before asking, "You're okay with me talking to some people about this? I'll leave your names out, of course."

"Yeah, please do. I need to make sure that after —" I swallow hard and continue. "—our time is over; he will be safe on his own."

She sucks her bottom lip into her mouth, her eyes squinting as she studies me. "You like him. Like genuinely really like him."

"Oh, stop that." I shoo her nosiness away.

"You didn't deny it." She gasps, my name a breathy exhale. "*Vivian.*"

"Autumn." My tone is far more of a scold.

"You seem happier since you met him, you know," she murmurs. "I think it's high time that you focus on your own happiness for once. And put yourself first."

Her words sink into me, and I consider them carefully. But until we know what I did to Greyson, I'm not even contemplating the idea that we could be more after this is over.

"Oh, fine. I'll bug you about it later." She rolls her eyes. "But trust me, I won't forget. How much longer do you two have together?"

"A little over a week," I answer as the door behind me opens and a couple of customers walk in. *Humans.* Reaching forward, I pluck the pen from her hand and scribble my number on the paper while smiling at the new customers. "Call me when you find something."

"Of course," she mumbles before addressing the cute couple. "Good morning, guys!"

They fall into conversation, but I don't bother

listening to their small talk as I drop the pen on the counter and stride out of the shop.

I'm sure that Greyson will be totally fine and nothing too crazy is going on. Yeah. I'm sure of it.

But I don't have to tap into my own emotions to know I'm lying to myself; I can tell that by the baseball-size knot in my stomach. If whatever is happening puts him at risk, I'm not letting him leave my house, whether he likes it or not.

After finishing my errands and clearing my head, I return home, feeling Greyson's presence the second I pull into the driveway. It's like he's unlocked a new sense in my body that is only tuned in to him.

By the time I walk through the front door, I can feel his emotions so deeply in my veins I can't tell where his end and mine begin. *Excitement. Adrenaline. Anticipation.*

What is he doing right now?

Tapping into my hearing, I search the house for any noise, and I can't help but giggle when the only sound I find is the turning of pages in a book.

He's reading.

It's fascinating that the emotions he's experiencing right now seem as real as the ones he feels in real life.

"Honey, I'm home!" I call through the house in a bright and playful tone as I kick my shoes off and walk into the main room.

Greyson chuckles from the living room, and as I turn the corner, I see him toss a throw blanket off his lap as he rises to his feet and starts walking toward me.

Fuck, I somehow forgot how much of a sexy, massive man he is. His white T-shirt is drawn taut across his chest and arms, doing little to hide the muscle he carefully crafts day in and day out.

His blond hair is tucked beneath a backward baseball cap, the tips of his light locks peeking out from beneath the material, and I don't know if he's ever looked hotter than he does at this very moment.

Each step toward me births a new butterfly in my stomach, and by the time he's only a few feet from me, they've evolved into bats that are desperately trying to break through my rib cage.

"I think this is my new favorite look for you." I swoon as he reaches forward, his fingers brushing against my waist.

"Sweats and a T-shirt?" He laughs and offers to take the bags from my hands.

"Details matter. Those gray sweats, a white T-shirt that is thin enough that I can almost see the outline of each ab on your stomach, and a backward cap. Don't forget the glasses either." Swallowing hard, I can't help but check out his back when he turns and walks toward the dining room table with the bags. "Fuck, yes, definitely never take this outfit off."

He turns around, a cocky grin on his face. "Never, hmm?"

Glaring at him, I scoff. "You know what I mean."

Speeding over to his side faster than the blink of an eye, I start unpacking the bags before he turns back toward the table.

"You went grocery shopping?" he asks, confused, his brows pinching together. "You don't eat food."

"I know that. They're for you. Your favorites." I smile, showing each item off before I set it down on the table.

He watches me carefully, his stare burning into me. "I could have done this, Vivian."

Shrugging, I grab a few things and walk over to the fridge in an effort to hide the blush creeping onto my cheeks. "I know, but I wanted to."

Opening the door, I unload my haul into the fridge. I don't know how far I'm willing to take this flirting. I like Greyson, I do, but his involvement with me makes him a target. If anyone hurts him…it would destroy me. And I don't know if I can survive that kind of pain again.

"*Shit.*" Spinning on my heels, I come face to chest with Greyson.

He smirks and cages me against the fridge with one arm as his other hand lifts my chin up. "Thank you."

"Y-Yeah, you're welcome. Gotta keep my bloodling fed well," I stutter. "It's no big deal."

He swallows hard. "It is to me." And pauses. "How can I return the favor?"

Ugh, I hate how nervous he is making me right now. I should push him away, put a little distance between us. But I can't. Everything in my body wants to be near him.

"Eat the food. That seems fair enough to me." I bite back my grin.

He raises his wrist to my lips. "Only if you do the same."

"Later," I whisper, gently pushing at his chest and sneaking beneath his arm pinned by my head.

"Are you running from me?" he snarks and scoffs. "You think you're too fast for me?"

Turning enough to glare at him, I laugh. "It's cute that you think you have any chance of catching me."

"Should we make a bet?" he challenges, squaring his shoulders up with me.

Shrugging, I spin on the ball of my foot, facing him fully. "If you win?"

"Then I get to devour my favorite sweet treat between your legs right here on this counter," he groans, stepping toward me and snaking his finger beneath the hem of my skirt. "If you win?"

A thousand ideas flash in my mind, all of which I desperately want to do in the confines of my bedroom. But I'm too on edge to relax after what Autumn said.

Glancing to the side, I spot Lucy walking into the room. "You take Lucy for a walk."

His brows furrow. "Does she like going on walks? Like on a leash?"

Lucy brushes against my leg before glancing up at me, her green eyes narrowing like she can hear me volunteering her for a walk, which she absolutely does not enjoy.

"Oh yeah," I lie through my teeth, "She loves them."

He studies me with suspicion. "How should we do this? On the count of three?"

By the time he finishes the last word of his question, I'm already standing halfway up the staircase before sitting and crossing my ankles.

Surprise widens his eyes as he searches for me,

finding me a few moments later, annoyance in his stare. "Oh, so you're cheating?"

Standing up, I brush my hands down the suede skirt. "Not at all. I was just using your blabbing to my advantage."

He strides, his long legs bringing him to the base of the stairs in seconds. "Yeah, exactly. *Cheating*."

"Are you going to catch me or not?" I sigh, pretending I couldn't be more bored.

He chuckles deeply and roughly. "You better run fast."

He digs his feet into the floor before charging up the stairs. I love his confidence, but it truly is wasted on this challenge. There is no world where he catches me unless I let him.

Turning, I race up the stairs, and within three seconds, I'm standing in my grand office, which has certainly seen better days when it wasn't covered in an inch of dust. Tapping into my hearing, I can tell Greyson is nearing the top of the stairs. He's fast. But I'm faster.

Running out of the room, I rush past Greyson, trailing my fingers across his torso as I pass, the wind from my speed whipping at his hair and clothes. I'm going to go to my bedroom, lead him in there, and then go back downstairs and wait for him in the kitchen. Might as well give him a nice little workout before I end our game.

My fangs fight to protrude from my gums, my power wanting to fully come out and play, but I keep it at bay.

Looping through my bedroom, I head back the way I came, racing past Greyson, gaining speed by the second as I descend two stairs. Something deep inside of me urges me to jump, to leap from the top of the stairs to the floor below.

An odd sensation courses through me, like a surge of power and strength from deep within surfaces for the first time. I don't recognize it, but I trust it anyway.

Kicking off the step, I launch myself into the air. *Holy shit!* It's like I'm flying. I soar high up through the sky-high room before gravity gradually pulls me down to the floor, ten feet further than I expected to land.

What the hell was that?

I didn't even know that was something I could do; I've never tried it. I mean, I've jumped insane distances when I could get a good running start, but nothing compared to what I just did.

"Woah! That's cool!" Greyson shouts from the top of the stairs, and as he meets my eyes, his face falters. "Your eyes are red. Are you hungry?"

My eyes never transform without my knowing, so the fact that they shifted without my realization is yet another thing to add to the damn list of weird shit going on.

"I mean, yeah," I say breathlessly and honestly as I take the two steps toward the kitchen counter and rest my palms against the cool surface. "I've never done that before."

He hurries down the stairs and stops at my side. "Really? Because you didn't know you could or just didn't try?"

"Both, I guess?" I shrug, feeling even more confused about everything going on.

"Wow, that's pretty amazing though. I wish you could have seen it from my eyes." He swoons. "It was beautiful. You looked so powerful. I ran around the corner, and you were thirty feet in the air, plummeting to the floor with your arms raised at your sides, your palms up to the ceiling. But you weren't falling in a scary way like you were going to get hurt. It was controlled and intentional. It was…" His eyes darken. "…kind of hot."

My cheeks warm from his compliment, part of me loving how giddy he makes me feel and the other part of me wishing that he would stop being so damn sweet.

Forcing myself to keep him an emotional distance

away, I murmur, "I suppose we should set some boundaries."

"You want to do that *now*? After I've already been buried inside of you? I think we already broke all of the boundaries." He laughs, and I find it endearingly annoying that I find even his laugh can be so attractive.

Rolling my eyes, I tap my fingers on the counter incessantly. "I mean for when this is over. It's a contractual agreement. Once our time is up, we part ways and go back to our separate lives."

My senses have been open to him all day, and I can't help but notice the ache of pain from my words, like he got punched in the gut.

But I remind myself that it's easier this way. Safer.

His words are cold while he smiles, pretending to hide his discomfort, but I can feel it deep in my bones. "I understand. That's probably for the best."

He knows this is temporary. I can live with ignoring the feelings growing between us as long as he's safe.

I'm also tired of all of these conflicting feelings. I'm over it. I never should have bid on Greyson at the Culling. And then none of this would be happening. But even the thought makes my stomach twist because there is some part of me deep down that wants to be near him, no matter the risks.

The room gets hotter as my mind spins with everything going on. This was complicated enough with me publicly taking a bloodling. But now…ugh, it's turning into something bigger, and I worry that I'm losing control, the last thing that's supposed to happen right now.

The hair on the back of my neck rises. Opening my senses up, I search for the source, as if hundreds of invisible tendrils are stretching out from me, seeking the emotion of whoever or whatever has arrived.

Oddly, I'm thankful for the distraction from the mood-killing conversation I started.

"Someone's here," I murmur, pushing away from the kitchen counter and strolling over to the door.

I don't recognize who it is, or rather who *they* are. Two of them. Young.

When I pull the door open, my gaze falls feet lower to two little girls in green vests pulling a wagon of boxed cookies. "Hi! Would you like to buy some Girl Scout cookies? We're trying to raise money to go on a vacation."

The other little girl slaps her arm lightly. "You're supposed to say a trip, not vacation."

They immediately remind me of me and Genevieve when we were younger. Her delicate blue eyes flash in my memory, slicing through my heart.

My senses reach two other humans. They're here, but they are further away, probably their parents waiting in the wings.

"How much do you guys have left to raise for the trip?" I ask softly, bending down at the waist to be at their level.

Their eyes go blank at my question. They have no idea, which is fair, I suppose, because they look like they are barely seven or eight years old.

"I'll take the whole wagon, then." I smile as their faces light up with uncontainable excitement.

"Really?" the little girl with dark hair squeals.

"I'll be right back," I tell her before walking inside to grab my wallet.

"Girl Scouts?" Greyson smiles sweetly, and I roll my eyes.

"Yes, Girl Scouts. I love…"

"Definitely not the cookies." He laughs.

"Their morals and the empowerment they give little girls." I lift my nose at him as I stride past him and grab my wallet before heading back to the happy entrepreneurs.

Besides, I can't help but recall the dreams I once

had of being a mother. The backs of my eyes burn, but I blink the wetness away. That dream isn't entirely impossible for vampires, but only under rare conditions can a vampire conceive. I don't know if there are any documented human-and-vampire-born children. Regardless, those options aren't possible for me. If I won't keep anyone around for fear of their life, I certainly won't bring a child into the mix.

Opening the door, I find them haphazardly stuffing the tens of boxes into bags. "How much do I owe you?" Deciding to help them out with the math part of this transaction, I grab the clipboard and calculate it myself.

Each box is six dollars. And I'm getting...one hundred and twenty-three boxes. I do the math in my head. Seven hundred and twenty-eight dollars.

Taking ten hundred dollar bills from my wallet, I hand it over. "Here's one thousand dollars. Keep the change, and have the best trip ever!"

"Are you sure?" The blonde girl beams with happiness. "We raised the most out of any group now!"

"Awesome! I'm glad I could help." I grin and start grabbing bags from the ground. "Is one of your parents here?"

"Mom!" Little blondie calls out, and a brunette

woman emerges from behind the tall hedges left of my walkway, her head popping out so quickly it nearly startles me. And I laugh at the fact that a human caught me off guard with her quickness.

"Right here!" she cheers. "How are we doing?"

"This nice lady is buying all of the cookies! She gave us a thousand dollars!" she squeals.

"Wow, Anna! Great job, you two!" She speaks to them in that tone of voice reserved just for kids before turning her attention to me, her voice now normal. "Thank you so much for purchasing so many boxes. It means the world to these girls. Can I get you anything else? Need help carrying them inside?"

Grinning, I flash her a smile. "I think we'll be okay. Thank you though. And I'm happy to help. Let me drop these inside. I'll be right back."

"Of course!" She beams.

Rushing back inside, I drop the armfuls of bags onto the kitchen counter while Greyson eyes me, a shit-eating grin on his face. "Need a hand?"

"Nope," I huff, fighting back a laugh.

The mom is gone when I return, and I grab the rest of the cookies. "Thank you guys for bagging these up for me."

"You're welcome," they say in unison.

As I turn to walk back inside the house, I glance once more at the two cuties for one last smile goodbye. But that happiness pouring off them is quickly replaced by bone-chilling fear.

"What's wrong?" I ask, rushing back over to them and dropping to my knees.

They jump back and point at me, and the dark haired girl gasps. "You're a monster!"

My heart drops. "W-What?"

"Y-Your e-eyes a-a-are r-red," she gasps, her voice almost inaudible.

Shit.

Without wasting a second, I latch onto both of their minds and tell them, "Forget about my red eye color and leave."

They nod mindlessly as they grab the wagon and walk away. Hurriedly, I gather the dropped bags and rush inside, slamming the door behind me and sliding down onto the floor.

For just a moment, I wasn't Vivian Barlowe, vampire. I was just Vivian, imagining what it would be like to have a little girl of my own. And then I watched their admiration change in front of my eyes to utmost terror.

I spent so long making sure that I was in control of my life, my power, and those around me. No one has the capability to truly surprise me or hurt me anymore. I made sure of that, and I've succeeded for decades. But now, everything is changing, and I hate not knowing how or why. I've never felt more out of control.

"Hey, are you okay?" Greyson rushes over to me, crouching down and cupping my face.

"I-I don't know." My gaze meets his as my eyes burn, and tears fall down my cheeks.

Chapter Eleven
greyson

It's been two days since Vivian scared the little girl scouts and filled me in on the truth of what's been happening, although she doesn't have any of the actual answers. She told me how impossible it is that her energy is laced with mine. She and Autumn have been desperately searching for an answer, but they've yet to discover anything to tell us why.

We've been damn near inseparable the last couple of days. She's been feeding on me regularly, without the sex. Which I honestly haven't minded. The desire is present tenfold when she feeds, but even without the sex, it's incredibly intimate.

Don't get me wrong, I love fucking her. But getting to know her, getting past the persona of power and sex appeal, and seeing pieces of the vulnerable woman that lies beneath has been *everything*.

I can tell there's more she isn't telling me; I can hear it in the silence between her words. I wish she would trust me, but I can understand why she doesn't. In terms of her life, she's known me for such a minuscule amount of time. But that doesn't make it sting any less that she's holding something back.

She left early this morning to meet with the High Council, but I have no idea what it's about, nor if it's any of my business. But part of me has an inkling that it has to do with Vivian and me. She told me not to wait around for her today because she wasn't sure when she would be back.

Lucy and I spent the majority of the morning watching TV together, cuddled up on the couch. She is officially my best friend. Then I took her on a walk. Vivian said she likes her harness and going outside, but Lucy would disagree with that statement if our walk this morning proves anything. Leaving Vivian after this is one thing; leaving Lucy, my little Lulu, behind too is another pain entirely.

We only have five days left together per our agreement, but it doesn't feel like enough. I'm not ready to say goodbye. I've never met anyone like Vivian, and I don't just mean the fact that she's a vampire.

She comes across as rather serious yet playful, a girl who is always smiling when others are present, even if she doesn't feel that way inside.

That's just the version of herself she shows the world. Behind the cheery mask is a girl who has a lot of story and pain. She hides those parts of herself so well. If I didn't study her so intently all of the time, and if I didn't have those parts of myself, I would never have noticed the slight cracks in the foundation.

I want her to know that she doesn't have to lift that pain alone; I can take some of it too. I can't imagine the life of a vampire is an easy one. Living in secret from the rest of the world while trying to blend in with everyone else, it has to be exhausting.

She doesn't have to shy away from her true self around me. She can just be. I find her red eyes just as beautiful as I do her hazel ones, her strength just as breathtaking as her weakness.

Besides, I think her fangs are hot as hell.

I got into this agreement for the money, but I don't know if I can take it, knowing that afterward, I walk away from her. It's like I've been running on autopilot my entire life, only waking up after I met her.

How do I tell her all of this without scaring her away?

I know she feels the connection between us as much as I do, like a tangible tether tying us together. She has to. Even if she does, she might not want to pursue anything further. But I don't want this to end.

Granted, I could probably enter the Culling again in six months, and she would likely bid on me, but the thought of her not choosing me or going that long without seeing her makes my heart constrict in my chest.

This could all be made up in my head, a story that I desperately want to believe in. Even if this is all a fantasy in my mind, I hope I never find reality again.

My phone dings, pulling me from my thoughts, and I glance at it, finding a text from Steven.

> Steven: Rent is due tomorrow. I need your half.

God, I've been living in peace the last week that I forgot how much I fucking hate Steven.

I can't believe that I ever agreed to move in with that dumbass. I don't care if Vivian kicks me to the curb when this is all said and done, I'm not going back to that damn apartment.

I have enough money now to buy out my half of

the six-month lease, and that's exactly what I'm going to do.

> On my way to drop it off.

Within minutes, I'm on my way to the bank to withdraw all of the money I need to get Steven the hell out of my life. We have two months left on our six-month lease, and all I have to do is pay my half of the rent for this month and the next two.

I'm just going to throw the few possessions I still have at the apartment into a duffle bag, and then I'm out of there. I'm not going to even bother taking the furniture with me. He can sell it for all I care.

I arrive within ten minutes, throwing my car in park and rushing up the stairs of the building to unit 4E. After a minute of fighting with the key in the door, I push it open and find Steven watching me from the living room couch. He could have at least gotten off of his ass to let me in when he heard the lock struggling. But I'm not surprised.

"Wow, you're still alive," he mumbles, his attention shifting back to the TV.

Wasting neither of our time, I get straight to the point. "I'm moving out. I'm just here to drop off rent and grab my stuff."

His eyes widen, and he sits up taller, a dumb smile

on his lips that is begging to be punched off his face. "You are?"

"Great job containing your excitement," I grumble as I walk across the floor toward my bedroom, making a pit stop by the couch as I count the two thousand dollars out and drop it into Steven's lap. "There you go."

"T-Thanks," he murmurs as I walk away.

As I throw my bedroom door open, a wave of anger washes over me. Long gone is the patience that I once had for him. "What the fuck, Steven!"

"Shit, I forgot to clean up in there." He rubs the back of his head, no empathy or regret in any of his features.

Rather, he's annoyed that I caught it at all.

"Why would you need to clean it? You know the only rule I had was that no one could come into my room. Let alone my goddamn bed," I groan as I grab my duffle bag from the closet and quickly throw the only things I care about into it before storming out of the room. "The rest is yours. Congrats. Go fuck yourself, Steven."

He rises to his feet and hobbles over, probably drunk out of his mind from the odor wafting my way. Even though it's barely six o'clock. "Fuck you, Greyson! Always thinking you're better than everyone else."

"I've never said that," I correct him.

"There's no way your girlfriend isn't an uptight bitch for having to deal with you—"

Rearing my arm back, I follow through with my punch, burying my fist into his face. "Don't." I hit him again. "Ever." And again. "Say a word about her." One final hit is all I need to drop him to the ground.

"I'm sorry! I'm sorry!" He holds up his hands, and I can't help but take a mental image of his helpless gaze and whimper. "Shit, man."

Scoffing, I grab my bag and throw it over my shoulder before storming out of the apartment, slamming the door behind me as adrenaline pumps through my veins.

Holy shit. I should have done that a long time ago.

By the time I slide into my car, I still have yet to hear back from Vivian. I'm not ready to go back to her place yet. I haven't done anything in days except to lounge around. The fresh air is nice.

Besides, Lulu deserves some new toys and treats. I'm going to grab a few things for her and maybe some beautiful flowers for Vivian. I want to put a smile on my girls' faces.

My trip to the pet store was quick but definitely not cheap. It's not my fault though; I couldn't decide what to get her, so I got everything that caught my eye. Now, I want to stop and get Vivian some flowers.

I pull over next to Ambrose Floral and step out of my car, walking on the cobblestone sidewalk to the entrance. The place is bursting with flowers and plants, the aroma almost too refreshing, making me sneeze when I take a quick breath.

"Hi, can I help you with anything?" a sweet older woman asks me. "Bless you, by the way."

I grin. "Thank you. And I'm looking to get a couple dozen red roses. They're romantic flowers, right?"

She eyes me sweetly, a twinkle sparkling in her gaze. "Yes, very romantic. They are a favorite for those looking to impress someone."

Digging my wallet out of my back pocket, I grab my wallet and meet her at the counter. "Perfect. I'll take two dozen."

"You got it." She rings it up and leaves me to pay while she fetches the flowers and wraps them up in a bouquet.

Tapping my card on the reader, I pay and leave a generous tip. "Thank you so much."

"Come back anytime. I'm certain that whomever you got these for will love them."

Nodding her way, I walk back out to the car, gently tucking the bundle in the back seat before opening my driver's-side door. But right before I'm about to slide inside, a glowing sign catches my eye across the street.

Glancing up, I read the name set aside a crescent moon in a neon sign. Hale Bar.

I'm not much of a drinker by any means. I couldn't even tell you the last time I had a beverage with alcohol in it.

Greyson from two weeks ago would laugh at the idea of going to a random bar and drinking by myself in the evening. But I don't even know if I'd recognize that version of myself anymore.

Fuck it.

Shutting the door, I lock my car with my keys before carefully jogging across the street toward the rustic brick bar, slowing down as I reach the wooden door at the entrance.

Stepping inside, I immediately love the vibe. Dark navy blues, grays, and blacks decorate the interior. Even the pool table is blue with dark stained wood. It reminds me of a bar I would see in an old movie, where a cloud of cigarette smoke would hang in the air. But thankfully, no one is smoking inside tonight.

Descending the few stairs to the main floor, I can't help but feel eyes all over me as I cross the hardwood to the light wood bar and sit down on an empty stool.

A guy a few chairs down blatantly stares at me with a look of confusion and something else I don't quite understand.

"What can I get started for you?" a deep, rough voice cuts through the music. The bartender is rocking a black-and-gray flannel over a white T-shirt with a short beard.

To be honest, I don't even know what I like. The handful of times I've gone out, I usually just order the same as the people I'm with.

Cracking my knuckles beneath the edge of the countertop, I ask, "Is it weird if I ask you to surprise me?"

He chuckles deeply. "Not at all. I'll bring you something that'll really take the edge off."

"Sounds great. Thanks," I respond as he grabs a glass and begins pouring a few different liquids together.

Pulling my phone out, I shoot Vivian a quick text.

> Hey, hope everything's okay. I was out running a few errands and decided to stop for a drink quickly. I'll be back soon

Setting my phone down on the counter, I spin it in circles, holding it lightly in place with my finger, repeating it over and over while my mind drifts to places it probably shouldn't be. Ones where Vivian is sprawled out beneath me, laid bare for only my eyes to see.

Our time together is almost up. And I'm going to have to tell her sooner or later that I like her, that I don't want to lose her. The thought of it scares me more than finding out that vampires and witches exist.

"Here you go." The bartender slides a tall glass with an interesting-colored liquid over to me.

"Thanks," I murmur, picking the glass up and taking a sip, nearly spitting it back into the glass.

It's not bad. It's just...weird and very strong. I've never tasted anything like this.

It's got hints of blood orange and mint with some other bizarre flavor that I don't recognize.

"Do you like it?" he asks, and I don't miss the slight humor in his smile.

"Y-Yeah. It's good. What's in it?" I ask, taking

another drink that, of course, goes down the wrong tube, making me cough obnoxiously.

He laughs loudly at my pain, flatting his palms against the edge of the barside countertop. "A few different liquors, herbs, juices, and our secret house mix."

"I've never had anything like it, that's for sure," I say truthfully, making a mental note to never ask a bartender to surprise me again. I've only had, like, three drinks, and I can feel it hitting my bloodstream. "It's definitely strong."

"Oh yeah, you'll be feeling it soon. Got to get you your money's worth. Although this one is on the house tonight. I haven't seen you around before, and the first drink is free to new customers." He grabs a rag and tosses it over his shoulder.

Lifting the cool glass to my lips, I take another drink. "You must work a lot to know everyone that comes in here."

He shrugs and sticks his hand out. "I'm Lachlan Hale. This is my bar. And if our doors are open, you can usually find me right here."

Shaking his hand, I try to match his strength, but fuck, it's like he's trying to break my bones. "I'm Greyson Gilmore. Nice to meet you."

I'm not too sure why I gave him my last name,

but I guess I was trying to mirror my answer to his subconsciously.

"Nice to meet you, man. Have fun tonight. It will definitely be one to remember," he scoffs with a cocky grin before walking away.

"What does that mea—? *Woah.*" As if a switch is flicked inside of my head, everything becomes fuzzy—my hearing, sight, touch. Like a thin, tingling cloud surrounds me.

Did he drug my drink? Oh well. Who cares?

All I know is that I feel like I'm floating right now. My head rolls back as my eyes glance up at the ceiling, the stars and moon spinning around for me. Wow, that's a cool trick.

Sitting up enough to grab my glass, I take a few more drinks, loving the euphoria that's coursing through me with every sip.

I wish Vivian were here for this, feeling as incredible as I do right now.

Blinking hard a few times, I look back up at the navy blue, starry night painted on the ceiling, watching the stars and moon dance across the sky.

After a few seconds, I glance down at my drink, ready for another gulp. But it's empty.

Did I finish it? Well, it couldn't have finished itself.

"How's it going over here? Enjoying yourself?"

Lachlan asks, a shit-eating grin on his face. "Do you want another one? I have to cut you off after this next one though. I only allow first-timers to drink three. When you consume four doses, it becomes dangerous."

"Three? Four? I barely finished my first one," I slur, my voice surprising me as I struggle to hold the man's stare.

It's blurry, like he's moving too quickly for my eyes to keep locked onto. Or maybe it's me that's rocking side to side.

A bubbling laughter leaves him. "Buddy, you already downed your second one. Maybe two should be your limit for tonight."

When the hell did that happen?

Some song plays loudly near me, and I can't figure out what it is until I hear the bartender answer the phone, and I realize it was the ringtone blaring in my ears. "Hale Bar." He pauses. "Don't worry. He's just fine. I was having a little fun." He pauses again, chuckling. "Yeah, see you in a few."

He hangs the call up as I reach out and slap my hands on the counter to stop myself from falling backward off the stool.

I want to ask him who was on the phone, but as I part my lips to say the words, I forget what I'm doing.

Maybe I should call Vivian. God, I miss her so much.

A loud bang sounds behind me, and I spin too fast for my eyeballs to keep up as I try to find the source of the sound.

A fuzzy outline that resembles Vivian appears in the entrance of the bar, and a voice that sounds just like hers cuts through all of the noise, growing louder by each second. "Lachlan Hale, you son of a bitch. What did you do?"

I blink and she appears next to me, her delicious scent seeping into every pore of my body as I breathe her in.

Her name is barely a whisper on my lips. "Vivian."

She rubs her hand up and down on my back. "I leave you alone for five minutes, and you stumble into a werewolf bar. You are drawn toward danger, Greyson, I swear." She giggles.

She steps closer to the counter, eyeing Lachlan up. "Thank you for keeping an eye on him. But also screw you for giving him that drink, you shithead."

Lachlan holds his hands up in defeat. "I smelled your scent on him the second he walked in. I couldn't help myself. Sorry."

She scoffs, "No you're not."

Immediately, he says, "No, I'm not." And laughs. "Greyson, it was great meeting you."

"Let's go," she murmurs to me, her warm voice wrapping around me like a blanket.

"Yeah. A-Anywhere with you," I slur and grab her face, kissing her cheek.

Blinking a few times, I feel cold air on my arms, and as I open my eyes, I'm standing next to my car, Vivian holding the passenger door open for me.

Jesus, these time jumps are discombobulating.

She ushers me in, and I slump into the seat. A millisecond later, she's behind the wheel and starting the car.

"God, why does it smell like roses in here?" she sneers, sounding disgusted.

"For you. God, I missed you," I groan.

Even though I barely know where I'm at and seem to be losing time, I don't miss the blush that spreads on her cheeks from my words.

"I missed you too, Grey," she murmurs softly, almost too quiet for me to hear.

My thoughts fluidly flow from my mind to my lips, and even if I try to stop it, I can't help but speak them into existence. "You have no idea what you're doing to me, Vivian. I like you so much. I don't want to walk away from you. Tell me I don't have to." I pause, waiting for her to say something as she pulls away from the curb, but she doesn't, so I fill the void effortlessly.

"You're so beautiful. Every single inch of you leaves me fucking breathless. Please, say something. Tell me to shut up. Tell me you don't want me to stay. Tell me anything."

She remains quiet, her brows furrowing as her lips part, like she can't decide whether to tell me something or not.

Her next words leave me breathless for a whole other reason. "I'm scared that if I keep letting you in, your fate will be the same as Genevieve's."

"Vivian" I exhale. "I'm so sorry."

She wipes a tear from her lashes. "It was a very long time ago."

Reaching out and brushing her hair back so I can better see her face, I murmur, "I'm right here and I'm not going anywhere."

A painful smile flashes on her lips. "I'll do whatever it takes to keep you out of harm's way. Besides, you won't remember this conversation anyway. Not from the amount of wolf-ale he gave you.

"I'll always remember everything when it comes to you." Resting my hand across her thigh, I stroke my thumb back and forth.

"Are you happy with the life you're building?" she

asks, the complete topic change and seriousness of her question catching me off guard.

I don't think I could lie to her right now if I tried. "No." I take a deep, shaky breath. "Not anymore."

"Why?" she whispers, glancing over at me so quickly I almost don't catch it.

I don't know what that guy gave me, but it's like it removed every filter from my body, every thought immediately leaving my lips.

We pull into her long, winding private driveway, and she kills the engine when we pull up to the house.

"I went into finance because I knew it would provide a good financial and stable future. But even though I'm good at it, I hate it. But I chose a path that would be safe because that's all I wanted growing up. It was Cheryl's dream for me to do this and I worked tirelessly to honor that."

"She would be proud of you, Grey." She takes a shaky breath. "Let's get you inside," she murmurs before disappearing and popping up outside of my car door, pulling it open.

Stepping out, I wobble back and forth, trying to find my footing but failing miserably.

A laugh bubbles out of her. "This is going to be a lot easier my way. Just relax."

"What do you mean? *Ahh!*" I gasp as she scoops me up into her arms bridal style.

"Hold on tight," she smirks before the world around me becomes nothing but one big blur. "Here we are."

She sets me down on the floor of our bedroom, and I try not to vomit everywhere from the whiplash she just gave me.

"Easy, just sit down. You'll settle in a moment," she says, guiding me back onto the bed.

She steps back, but I stop her, grabbing her hand and tugging her toward me. She tumbles on top of me, her face stopping inches from mine, her warm breath drawing me closer.

The air seems to thicken around us, and I can't tear my gaze from her lips as our breathing begins to sync.

"You said you didn't want that life anymore," she whispers, sucking in a sharp breath before asking, "What do you want out of life now?"

I don't hesitate. There's only one thing that I know without a doubt I want. "You."

She smiles, her eyes twinkling as she scoffs happily. "You're ridiculous…and drunk."

"And yet I mean it anyways."

Reaching up, I brush her hair back with my hand,

cupping her jaw. "I've wasted so many years playing it safe, Vivian. I'm done. I want you. Only you."

"You do?" she asks, her tone of excitement and a twinge of sadness rolled into one.

Without thought, I pull her face down, claiming her lips with my own, proving to her just how much I mean what I said.

I only pull away enough to murmur, "You have no idea what you mean to me."

Plunging my tongue into her mouth, I pull her tighter against me, needing to be closer to her. "I'll do anything to stay with you. Turn me into a vampire, do anything to me that grants me forever by your side."

She kisses me ferociously, grinding her hips down onto me with delicious intent.

"*Greyson*," she gasps between kisses. "I want you too."

We melt together, our motions flowing together in perfect sync as our kiss deepens.

She pulls away and sighs. "You're going to pass out shortly. The drug in the ale has side effects. It's only a matter of time before you'll be out cold—"

Chapter Twelve
vivian

The last two days have been spent poring over books, trying to find any answer to the mystery of the connection between Greyson and me.

The things I feel for him terrify me to the bone. I was hoping my feelings were nothing more than lust and infatuation. But I know it's so much deeper than that, rooting itself in my heart and spreading further within me every day.

But it doesn't matter what book Autumn and I read through in the council's library; we can't figure anything out. I wish I could leave it be and brush it off, but coincidences and accidents don't exist in the paranormal world. There's more to it, I just know it.

I need to feed, which is the only reason I'm leaving Autumn to continue our search alone. During the feeding period, we should drink our fill each day for two weeks, but I already missed the last two days from being here. I'm starving.

Walking out of the doors of the Barlowe, I bump into Jason. "Hey."

"How's it going with the pairings? Everyone behaving themselves?" I inquire, feeling bad that I haven't checked in before now.

I'm usually much more hands-on during the Culling, but in my defense, I've never had Greyson with me before. He came into my life like a goddamn storm, changing everything in his path and sweeping me up in his along the way.

Jason nods. "So far, so good. No complaints from either side."

"Good to hear." I pat his arm as I stride past him. "I have to run, but I'll check in again soon."

Jason smiles kindly. "Sounds good. See you later, Vivian."

I've gotten lucky with the members I've chosen for the High Council over the years. I may have started this entire organization and hand-selected every staff member, but I've been lucky that there hasn't been a bad seed. It is a choice to be on the council but an honor nonetheless. We have had many members over the years that have served selflessly and went on to 'retire' from the role.

The High Council wasn't always this large of an operation. It started out as just me hunting down and killing vampires murderously preyed upon humans. And then a few other vampires that shared the same morals joined me. Eventually, our numbers doubled, tripled, multiplied out of control that we had to come up with some way to organize it all. The High Council was born.

My ability to alter the minds of humans and other vampires certainly played a role in peaking the interest of other's around us. My specific gifts had never been seen before and it earned a level of respect from countless vampires. Once they caught wind of the council we were building, they flocked to us, wanting to be a part of it.

The High Council selects well-rounded members of local councils to fill their seats. It's not democratic like the human world. There's no corruption or greed. Vampires sit on their council because they care for our laws. There is no profit to be made.

Vampires can come forward with complaints directly to their local presiding council, or they can come straight to the High Council if they wish. But there have been no major incidents, aside from a little lighthearted drama.

I have a feeling it has to do with the examples I set in the early years of the council's existence. Of course, back in the day, public executions weren't so crass, and they were welcomed by the community. It also set the tone. *Enough to sustain, never drain.* Our motto has never changed since it was first written in stone.

The rules are enforced regardless of who you are. If you break them, you are punished as deemed necessary by the High Council.

Even though we shy away from public executions now, we still punish those who violate the rules, but our methods have shifted to more modern alternatives. If anything, they've become more ruthless with the things we've learned.

A coffin made from white ash trees can make a vampire feel like they are losing their mind when they're buried beneath the ground. Line it with deadly nightshade, and it gives them horrific hallucinations as they breathe in the air around them.

Think of it as adult vampire time-out. Except at the end of their imprisonment, they don't get to return to their life; they are expunged from existence.

Unfortunately, there are still vampires that challenge us, but they never win that battle. Peace is all we've ever wanted, and our laws allow us just that. We won't let anyone get in the way of protecting everything we've built. The chaos and rage those monsters crave is the reason my best friend was drained so long ago. They wanted to knock me off a peg, show me how powerless I was. So they took her, tortured her, assaulted her, and drained her, leaving her at my doorstep afterward like a sick gift.

I made them pay. Each and every one of them suffered horrifically for decades before I tore them limb from limb and burned their bodies, turning them to nothing but ash.

Their very remains are concreted in the large clock tower in the Barlowe. A reminder to any who wish to cross me.

I miss Genevieve every single day. But I will make sure that her life is remembered. She is immortal, like Greyson said, even if it's only in my memories. She is the reason I started hunting rogue vampires in the first place and created what is now the High Council. One of the reasons the Culling even exists.

In a way, if it weren't for her, I may not have ever seen Greyson again. My heart beats hard in my chest at the thought.

I've been so focused on keeping humans an arm's length away, for fear of making connections and losing another person I care for.

My heart has stayed in the shadows for so long. I've forgotten how colorful and warm the world can be. It's all because of Greyson.

I'm baffled when it comes to him. He hasn't had an easy life. He's worked hard for everything he's earned. I understand better than anyone that sometimes the life you think you should have couldn't be further from the life you're meant to live. After Genevieve was drained, I swore to myself that I would never put a human at risk of that again. It destroyed me, ripped my heart out of my chest completely. I lost such a big part of myself the day she died.

Her eyes flash in my mind, and I suck in a sharp breath at the haunting vision. She was the kindest soul. She didn't deserve to die simply for loving me. I won't let Greyson meet the same fate.

They can try to hurt them, but they will pay with their lives, never able to leave a scratch on his perfect face. I will obliterate them, turn them into nothing.

Greyson makes me feel like I can emerge from the cage I've locked myself in. I feel connected to him physically, even when we're apart. As if I can feel him breathe, sense his emotions, hear his words whispered in the wind, we are tethered to one another somehow.

At first, I'll admit that I thought it had to do with

the feedings. Emotions can be magnified dramatically both for the human and the vampire, especially when the feelings already exist prior to the bite. But it can't create false emotions, only enhance them.

I've been drawn to Greyson since that first night in the bar. Even then, things happened that were unexplainable. Maybe we'll never find the answer or ever know why my energy is intertwined with his. Maybe there isn't an answer to discover at all.

But that is only one of the problems. Our arrangement ends tomorrow night. What am I going to do? What if he wants to leave?

After his drunken babble, I have a pretty good idea of how he feels about me, and as much as I'm scared to admit it, I don't want to lose him. He's the only person I've given pieces of myself to since Genevieve, and if he walks out, he's taking them with him.

Letting him stay is equally exciting and terrifying. But regardless of his choice, I won't let anyone hurt him. I'll keep him safe, whether from a distance or by his side.

As I pull into the long, winding driveway, I park next to Greyson's old, run-down car, remembering the gifts he got Lucy and me the other night. A laugh breaks past my lips.

Roses. I still can't believe he got me roses. The gesture and thought were sweet, but I can't stand the smell. I loved them when I was human, but as a vampire, they smell like rotting garbage. That's one part of vampire lore humans got right. We can't bear to be around that scent for too long. I love that he went out of his way for me, but I never want him to do it again.

Lucy, however, loves him for his generosity, happily accepting them. She's a bit of a spoiled princess, but to be fair, she deserves it. She's the sweetest little black kitty, and because I won't get to have her forever, I will make every day we have together extra special. And apparently, Greyson feels the same way with the four bags of toys and treats he got her.

As I walk up the steps of the house, the front door opens and Greyson steps out, wearing only black joggers and a backward cap. Holy Mother of Demons, I am never going to get used to seeing him.

I find it hard to believe that he truly flew under the radar all his life like he said because he's impossible not to notice. The kind of beauty and depth that people carve statues in honor of. Maybe I should add a large marble statue of Greyson to my collection of art, centering it in my foyer.

"Finally," he sighs with a smile tugging at his lips as he shuffles down the stairs to greet me.

Giggling as he leans down and kisses my forehead, I scoff. "I was only gone for two days."

He rolls his eyes. "Well, in the scheme of our time together, that's a lot."

My chest pains at the reminding thought that this could all come to an end tomorrow. "You're right. How can I possibly make it up to you?"

He smirks devilishly. "I have a few ideas."

Now it's me who's rolling my eyes. "I do need to feed again, especially since I didn't while I was gone."

"Were there no humans there willing to share?" he asks, offering his hand, which I happily accept, letting him guide me up the stairs.

"There certainly was." I pause, my gaze flicking to him as my cheeks warm. "But I have *particular* tastes."

"Mmm. Good to know." He pulls me inside and shuts the door before facing me and cocking his head to the side, exposing his jugular vein to me. "You better drink up, then."

Dropping my purse to the floor, I feel my fangs

begging to descend. "You should at least sit down and be comfortable."

Clicking his tongue, he reaches forward, sliding his hands around my ass and lifting me up, wrapping me around his waist. "You're right. We should get comfortable."

Running my finger along his jaw, I tip his chin up, forcing him to look at me. His heavenly blue eyes lock onto mine, holding my stare with breathtaking intensity.

Parting my lips, I try to speak, but nothing comes out.

He walks us around the couch, lowering himself to the cushion as I continue to straddle his lap.

"What do you want to do on your last full day as my bloodling?"

He shifts my weight into one hand before cupping my face with the other, his eyes darkening. "For you to get your fill. For you to mark every inch of me."

My core flutters at the thought.

"I'm yours, Vivian," he groans. "Do with me as you wish."

Tilting my head to the side, I lean forward, slowly parting his lips with my tongue before dipping it inside of his mouth. "Mmm. I like the sound of that"

He grabs my hips, his fingers claiming my body with his strength as his tongue dances with mine.

My fangs burst through their sheath, dying to sink into his neck. My hips roll against his, every nerve in my body coming alive from his touch as we fall into a tantalizing rhythm. His hands take control of my body, guiding me exactly where he wants me, and I happily oblige.

His tongue runs across my fang, drawing a drop of blood, and the second it hits my tongue, I can't help but moan at how good he tastes.

Pulling away, he leans back on the couch. "Drink from me, baby."

His chest rises and falls fast, his abs constricting with each breath. It is quite the mouthwatering sight to see. A drum pounds in my ears, the blood rushing through his veins calling out to me.

Inching forward, I wet my bottom lip as I slide my hand along his jaw and cock his head to the side.

With pleasure.

In one swift movement, I lash out, sinking my fangs into that silky, soft skin, his blood gushing into my mouth with fervor. My body rocks against his as I cradle his head in my hand, sucking and lapping my tongue on his neck, devouring him.

"Fuck, why does it feel so damn *good?*" he growls, grinding his hips up against me, and I can tell *exactly* how good it's making him feel.

Part of the euphoria comes from the bite itself, a

built-in sense of ecstasy to entice a willing human to want to come back for more. The other part has nothing to do with my fangs and everything to do with the way we feel about each other.

"Look at you, sucking me like a good little vampire." His voice is rough and ragged, sending relentless waves of pleasure to my core.

Grinding harder into him, I lap my tongue against his neck over and over, feeling goose bumps rise beneath his skin.

"Fuck, Vivian."

My body is on fire right now, every single cell begging to be touched and caressed by his wandering hands. I want more, I need more of him. Now. Tomorrow. Forever.

Unlatching my fangs from his neck, I feel trails of blood run down my chin as I sit up and meet his hooded stare.

He raises his fingers, swiping up one line of warm blood from my chin before holding it in front of my mouth. "Suck it clean."

Yes, fucking, sir.

Taking his finger into my mouth, I savor every drop of his blood, closing my eyes as I slide it out of my mouth, the suction popping upon release.

"Mmm," he hums, sucking his bottom lip into his mouth.

Leaning forward, I'm desperate to claim his lips with mine.

DING DONG.

The doorbell sounds through the house. Who the fuck is interrupting this right now?

I spring off of Greyson, appearing by the door a second later. I can feel her energy before I even see her—it's Autumn.

Opening the door, I take a quick breath before warning her, "This better be important, Autumn. I was right in the middle of something."

She mockingly wipes her chin, smiling. "Yeah, I can definitely see that."

Pressing my lips together, I try to stop the laugh from breaking free, but I fail. Wiping the remaining blood from my chin, I clean my hand as I ask her, "What are you doing here?"

I sense her worry and hesitation, making me feel the same way, completely on edge from her sudden arrival.

"Spit it out," I urge her, desperately wishing I could read her mind.

"I think I might have figured it out—the tether between you two." She takes a shaky breath.

Greyson's hand slides around my waist, pulling me into his bare chest.

Her stare bounces between Greyson and me. "I

can't believe I didn't think about it sooner. All of the signs were there..." She trails off before locking her gaze with mine, her eyes wide with disbelief. "This is going to sound crazy...but I think that you guys are the real life *lamia et fatis sanguis*."

"What is that?" Greyson murmurs into my ear, but I don't even know how to respond because my jaw is on the floor.

It's impossible, it's a myth. A vampire legend as old as time itself. *Lamia et fatis sanguis.* A Latin term loosely translating to *vampires and the blood of fate*.

Chapter Thirteen
greyson

Vivian invites Autumn inside, and we make our way to the living room, Lucy jumping up onto my lap and pushing against my hand for pets.

"It's impossible. Are you sure?" Vivian asks, her voice strained and chock-full of worry.

Raising my hand in the air, wondering why no one has yet to tell me anything, I ask, "Should I be concerned with whatever the hell is going on?"

"No." Autumn waves the question away with her hand. "Probably not." She pauses once more, cocking her head to the side. "To be determined."

"Autumn," Vivian scolds her. "Do you really think

that's what this is? I mean, the tale of *lamia et fatis sanguis* is just that, a story. Plucked from the pages of *The Book of Destiny*. Humans even know of the tale, creating movies and art to represent the two fated souls."

"Not exactly…" Autumn clicks her tongue. "I have a theory I want to test out. To see how deep the connection between you two goes."

"Like a quiz or…?" I ask, wishing for something simple, and Autumn shakes her head. Of course not. "Why do I get the feeling that I'm not going to like this?" I exhale, dragging my hand down my face.

"Because you probably won't," Autumn murmurs before glancing back at Vivian, a faint, humorous smirk dancing on her lips.

I don't know that I've ever seen Vivian so nervous before. It unnerves me that she's genuinely hesitant.

"How do we test it?" I ask flatly.

"From *The Book of Destiny*, it says that the two souls will recognize each other's…pain." Her apologetic stare darts my way, and I grimace

Scoffing, I toss my hands up, jokingly enthusiastic. "Great. Let's do it."

Vivian giggles nervously, and I glare at her for laughing at my soon-to-be pain.

"Are you open to trying it?" she asks me, resting her hand gently on my leg.

I'd do anything for her.

Nodding, I wonder if I'm going to regret this. "Yes. What do you need me to do?"

Autumn clasps her hands together, seeming far too excited about this. "Vivian, go somewhere else in the house. The furthest corner from here. And don't use that super hearing of yours."

Autumn disappears into the kitchen while Vivian holds my stare, waiting for my confirmation, and I nod, assuring her that I'm okay with whatever is about to happen. Her shy gaze falls to the floor, and a sweet, delicate smile lifts her lips right before she vanishes.

My heart rate spikes when Autumn walks back from the kitchen, wielding a sharp knife. "Don't freak out."

"What do you mean *don't freak out?*" I scoff at the audacity of her question. "You are not stabbing me with that," I protest, taking a step back.

She looks at me like I'm stupid. "Obviously I'm not going to *stab* you. I'm just going to cut your hand."

Strutting over to me, she seems eerily calm, like this is just a regular part of her day job. But I guess I don't know what a witch's typical day looks like. Maybe a big part of her job is going around cutting people.

"Which hand?" she asks, holding her right hand out between us.

The blade gleams in the light, and I stick out my right one, my non-dominant hand. "What's going to happen? Should I be nervous?"

She holds my stare as her eyes brighten, lighting up like a kid's on Christmas. "I know you're new to a lot of this, but if this works and proves that you guys are really *lamia et fatis sanguis*, it would be the most incredible thing to happen in vampire history. And I would be honored to simply bear witness to it."

Goose bumps erupt down my arms from her tone. "What are you testing with the knife?"

"If she can feel your physical pain or detect it in some way. A deep connection that doesn't exist between vampires and humans as we know it. It would mean that the legend has finally come true. And if she doesn't feel it, then we know that we're back to square one at trying to decipher why I feel her energy intertwined with yours."

Her gaze darts out to my hand, and she lifts my palm up to the ceiling.

Taking a quick breath, I blow it out, steadying and bracing myself. Pain isn't exactly new to me. I have scars scattered across my body from my youth to prove that.

"Do it," I tell her, sharply inhaling and holding my breath.

Carefully, she presses the knife against my palm.

"*Shit.*" I wince as she drags the sharp blade across my skin, and bright red liquid pools in my palm.

Vivian appears by my side before Autumn even lifts the blade from my wound. "Stop."

Wind blows against us as she slams to a stop, air whipping through the room from her speed.

She takes my hands in hers, concern etched into her features. "Are you okay?"

Autumn turns to Vivian. "Your deep worry is sweet and all, but we need to know. Did you feel it?"

Vivian clutches her hand to her chest, shaking her head ever so slightly. "Not exactly."

"What does that mean?" Autumn's brows furrow.

Gripping my wrist in one hand, Vivian unfurls her fist, holding it open next to mine.

She isn't bleeding, but stretching from one side of her palm to the other is a deep red mark. "I didn't feel the pain like you predicted. It was more like a tingling ache, and then this line appeared in its place."

Autumn jumps up and down, pure joy lighting her face up as she claps. "I might cry. This is the most amazing thing ever."

"I'm glad you're so excited about my pain." I

laugh. "I know you're thrilled about whatever is happening right now but what does it mean for us?" I ask genuinely because I have no idea what this means for my future or *our* future.

She looks between us with a smile that's taking over her entire face. "It means I was right about you two. And it's not a bad thing, unless you view great power and being granted the gift of finding your soulmate negatively."

My body warms at her mention of soulmates, and I want to ask a thousand questions, but I can't even get a word out. I don't know where to begin.

"You said you were reading about it?" Vivian asks Autumn, and I can see the wheels turning behind her eyes. "What else did you find out?"

We hang on to every word she says, "For starters, every time you feed on him, you grow stronger. In ways that no other vampire can. If you're not already, your power will begin to mutate, you'll grow stronger and faster. I imagine it will impact your abilities as well. We just won't know exactly how they're affected until it happens."

"You said we're soulmates?" The question is barely audible as it finally pushes past my lips, my heart stuck in my throat.

Vivian's gaze flicks my way, her stare soft, delicate,

and vulnerable. "Do you know what the term *lamia et fatis sanguis* means?"

I shake my head.

"It's Latin, translating to *vampires and the blood of fate.*" Her cheeks flush, and it makes me want to grab her face and kiss her senseless.

My nerves are standing on edge as she holds my gaze with her burning stare.

She releases my hand, and I throw my arm over her shoulders, pulling her into my side, right where she belongs.

Autumn's phone chimes, cutting through the tension in the room as she checks the message. "Crap, I have to get going. I have to go to the shop, but keep me updated if anything weird happens. I'll call you after I'm done."

"Sounds good," Vivian says before Autumn rushes out of the door, not even bothering to close it. But a second later, as if a large gust of wind blows through the foyer, the door slams shut seemingly of its own accord.

Silence stretches between Vivian and me as we wait for the other to speak first.

Reaching out with both hands, I tuck her hair back behind her ears, positioning myself toe to toe with her. "What does this mean? For…us?"

She wets her lips, a twinkle gleaming in her stare. "What do you want it to mean?"

Huffing, I bite down on my bottom lip. That was the last thing I was expecting. For her to offer me the control. She likes being in charge, and I don't mind it one bit. But I like knowing she wants my opinion, that she cares for my desires as much as her own.

She's the most selfless and kind person I've ever met. She locked herself away from the world for so long I can't believe that we found each other.

Does she want my reassurance?

Was my confession in the car the other night not enough to show her how badly I want to be with her?

"We're destined for one another, right? Already intertwined together in unimaginable ways?" I murmur, tilting her chin up and forcing her light golden stare to meet mine. I want to be lost in those beautiful eyes when I remind her exactly what I want.

She nods, her gaze searches my face, and she holds her breath as we teeter on the edge of dreamed potential and spoken confessions.

I stroke my thumbs over her cheeks, my fingers sliding into her loosely curled hair.

I want her to answer one question for me before I bare my soul to her, to lead her to the edge of the cliff with me before I dive headfirst, past the point of no return. "Do you want me to leave tomorrow? When we wake and our agreement officially ends, do you want me to go?"

She freezes beneath my touch, taken aback by my question, looking more fragile than I've ever seen her. Like the armor around her is finally cracking apart, and my vulnerable girl steps through.

The second I feel her head shake from left to right in my hands, everything inside of me snaps, like her slightest confession rips the iron bars off my heart, once and for all.

My gaze falls to her lips as fireworks erupt in my chest. I wish I could feel her emotions the way she can feel mine. *Does she crave my touch as much as I crave hers? Is she falling for me as hard as I am for her?*

Her breathing shallows out, and I don't have to have her gift to know how nervous she is right now. I can see the quickness of her breaths and the quiver of her bottom lip.

"*Good.* Because I don't ever want to leave." Tilting her head back, I crush my lips to hers, savoring her taste, and the moment my tongue swipes against her velvet lips, she snaps, kissing me back feverishly, like my kiss is what she needs to feed on to survive.

My hands fall to her waist, pulling her into me as I give my heart over with every single kiss and touch.

She pulls away, her reddened stare locking onto mine, but they aren't hazel; they're red.

It's not hunger that changes her eyes this time… it's passion. "I don't want to pressure you into staying."

I inch forward, her warm breath caressing my parted lips. "Baby, listen to me. You would have to drag me away from you to get me to leave." I pause, my forehead falling against hers as I recall everything I said to her in my car. "The night you picked me up from Hale Bar, do you remember what I said?"

She grins, her cheeks flushing that perfect shade of deep red. "I couldn't forget if I tried. But I didn't expect…" She trails off, and I recite her words from that night.

"For what? For me to remember?" I grab her chin and jaw with one hand, my lips brushing against hers, my voice rough with intensity. "I remember it *all*. I meant every word I said to you that night. Every single one. I'm yours, Vivian. For as long as you'll have me."

She purses her lips together. "And if I want you for forever?"

Claiming her lips with mine once more, I murmur, "If there's a way for me to live forever, then I'll be yours even then."

Her eyes sparkle, squinting at me like she knows

something I don't. But my guess is there's a lot that she knows that I have yet to discover about this world.

She smirks, that arrogant gleam in her eyes that I love shining brightly. "Don't speak too soon, Grey. There are definitely ways to make you immortal."

"By making me like you?" I ask, curiosity getting the better of me.

Of course it's crossed my mind, but I don't even know how it all works.

She nods, "Yes, or you can remain as you are, and still be granted immortality. Then I could drink from you indefinitely and we wouldn't have to find humans of our own to feed on. There are a bunch of ways to keep you around forever."

"Tell me about them." Sliding my hands around her side, I cup her ass and lift her to my waist as she yelps. "But first, we have some business to attend to."

She giggles as I carry her to the staircase, heading straight for our bedroom.

"You need to feed," I tell her, slapping her ass as we reach the top of the stairs, palming it in my hand, the sting of the cut pulsing straight to my dick.

As we walk into the bedroom, I can feel the desperation in her stare and the delicate yet intentional touch of her fingers that are trailing down the back of my neck.

She purrs. "Such a thoughtful soulmate."

I was never one to believe in fate growing up. If some powerful entity or source were guiding my life, then why was my fate to suffer at the hands of others my entire childhood?

I didn't want to believe it—until now. Until this very moment. Soulmates. Fated love. Meant to be. I never considered that I would experience it. That it existed at all. If I had been asked a month ago if I thought I would one day find my *soulmate*, I would have laughed.

But that was before Vivian. It's like everything in my life is measured by her presence. Before and after her. Everything in my life before I met her was cold, calculated, and colorless.

Since then, she's taken over every thought in my head and beat of my heart. She changed everything in ways I never could have imagined, and I never want to go back to the way things were before. I meant what I said…I'm hers. Whether she wants me or not, my heart forever hers.

I don't know if it's because of the fated vampire and blood connection that we latched onto each other so quickly and deeply or what, but I'm not going to question it.

I'm done analyzing every move I make before I take a step forward. To hell with the thought that we're moving too fast—that's the human doubt voicing its unwanted opinion.

All I know is that I love who I am when I'm with her. She makes me feel like I matter, like she sees me in a way no one ever has or will.

When my legs hit the bed, I bend over and lower her down, sucking in a sharp breath. I'm never going to get over how beautiful she is, like every inch of her being was created to be worshiped by me.

Her tongue slides into my mouth before I realize she even moved, and it takes me all but a second to react, kissing her back feverishly.

We become a blur of intense desire and uncontrollable passion. She tears her shirt down the middle, ripping it apart and tossing it to the floor. The rest of her clothes seem to disintegrate from her body seconds later as she moves faster than my eyes can keep up with.

Her hands thread into my hair, my baseball cap falling to join the graveyard of clothes on the ground, quickly followed by my sweats and my shirt. She spins us around, gently pushing at my chest, and I fall back onto the bed, moving myself further back as she drops onto her knees on the mattress.

She crawls to me, swaying her hips back and forth as she moves up my body, my cock pulsing intensely, begging to be set free from the confines of my boxers.

I'm so goddamn hard as her nipples skim my chest and her mouth claims mine. As she pulls away, she smiles, her fangs biting down on her bottom lip, her eyes glowing red.

The sight of her naked on top of me right now, all vamped out, is driving me fucking insane…and she knows it.

Grinding my pelvis up against her bare center, I growl, "Bite me, Vivian. Drink from me while I bury myself deep inside of you, right where I fucking belong."

She lifts her hips in the air, and I shove my boxers down my thighs as my erection springs free, bouncing against her center and making my cock throb with anticipation.

"Fuck," I groan, wrapping my hand around my length and pumping myself base to tip, swiping it through her wetness and coating myself in her arousal.

Gliding my tip through her soaked center once more, I ease my tip inside of her, a grunt escaping my lips as I feel her tight pussy adjust to take me.

Sliding my free hand up her side, I pull her waist forward and down, her breasts flattening against my skin. She claims my lips with hers as she crashes forward, arching her back and taking me half an inch deeper. Wiggling her hips, the sensation is nearly enough to make me lose control and slam into her.

She nips at my lip, drawing blood that slowly drips down my chin, before she pulls away, eyeing it hungrily as she wets her bottom lip. Then, she lashes out, licking from my collarbone up to my jaw, lapping the runaway drops up with her tongue and moaning with satisfaction as she swallows my blood.

"Mmm, you taste *so* good," she whimpers as her nose brushes against mine.

"Take all you want, baby," I whisper into her mouth and turn my head to the side. "And I'll…" I pause, gripping her hips tightly, my fingers digging into the delicate flesh, and thrust upward, filling her to the brim all at once. She cries out in surprise and pleasure as she stretches around me. "I'll get my fill of your pretty little cunt," I grunt. "If that's even fucking possible."

"Don't hold back," she whispers against my neck before pressing a soft kiss against the invisible marks from her previous feedings, sending a warm, familiar shiver down my body.

Without warning, I do exactly what she asks. Grabbing her hips, I thrust upward at the same time I bring her ass down onto me, my dick plunging deeper inside of her.

"Ahh!" she cries out.

Lifting her, I slam her back down onto me, an incoherent moan leaving her lips right before I feel her fangs penetrate my neck.

"Fuck," I grunt at the sudden burst of pain, but it's never felt better as I roll my hips and plunge into her, my cock stroking her insides with every relentless thrust.

Feeling her suck from my neck is an otherworldly sensation, heightening every ounce of pleasure tenfold. I'm fucking drunk on her bite, and I never want to sober up.

With ease, I lift her up and circle her hips as I glide back inside of her. She moans, the sounds muffled against my skin as her fangs continue to draw blood from me.

The sounds of our bodies colliding together, mixed with her muffled moans, fill the room with the hottest sounds I've ever heard.

She starts tightening around my length. She's getting close, and I want to feel her pussy spasm on top of me more than I want to breathe.

"Take every fucking drop, and don't stop," I encourage her, feeling her center start to pulse around me. "Give it to me, Vivian. Right now, baby. I want to feel you fucking explode."

Her fangs leave me for a brief second as her cries,

her uncontrollable moans, sing into my ear. "Greyson, Greyson! Oh my fuck!"

"That's it. What a good girl coming that hard for me." Grabbing the back of her neck, I fist my hand in her hair and push her mouth back down against my neck. "Get your fill, baby."

But instead of biting into me again, she sits up, my cock still buried inside of her. When I twitch it, her eyes light up, and her hips buck ever so slightly.

"What? Are you done already?" I ask, my eyes hooded, my tone playful as I smirk.

She shrugs and glances anywhere but at me, her blush and smile giving her lie away immediately. "Yeah, I've had enough."

I thrust my hips upward, and her eyes roll to the back of her head as I sit us up, pressing my lips against her neck. Securing my arm around her waist, I fist my hand in her hair and tug her head down back toward her ass, earning a delicious whimper.

"You might have had enough to drink, but I have a suspicion you haven't had enough of *this*." With my fingers tangled in her locks, I tug her hair again at the same time I rock into her, over and over.

Her mouth falls open, and she whimpers as I move inside of her, buried to the hilt.

Freezing, I release her hair and lean back on the

bed, crossing my hands behind my head with a devilish smirk on my lips.

Let's see what she says now.

"What do you think you're doing?" she demands, frustration etched in her every feature.

Bucking my hips into her, I playfully sigh as she gasps. "You said you've had enough. I'm a gentleman—I don't want to push you to do anything you don't want to do."

She huffs and grunts, her red eyes squinted with annoyance as she crosses her arms over her perfect tits, pushing her bottom lip out in the perfect pout. "And *you* said you wouldn't hold back."

"Tell me you want more," I growl and grab her chin, pulling her toward me until her lips are hovering over mine as I roll my hips into her again. "I want to hear you say it."

"It seems someone is gaining confidence." She whispers her quiet observation that couldn't be more true. I'm not afraid to take what I want anymore, and the only thing I want now is her.

Inching forward, I kiss her before biting down on her bottom lip. "What can I say? I feel fucking invincible with my cock this deep inside of you."

"I don't think you could stop if you tried," she murmurs, challenging me.

I knew she would fight me head-on; she likes the

control. As much as I love her having it, I want to see her lose it. To willingly hand it over to me.

"You doubt my willpower," I accuse, continuing to grind my hips into her.

Fuck, I'm doubting it right now too. But I can't let her know that. Even if she can sense it. I've already gotten this far.

Releasing her hair, I wrap my hands around her round ass, slide my legs off the bed, and stand up, her arms circling around my neck and her legs wrapping around my waist.

"Ahh," she softly moans as I lift her up before dropping her back down on my cock.

"You don't want anymore? *Really?*" I bite the words out as I hold her in place, roll my hips back, and plunge back into her, stretching her and taking her deeper than before.

"I don't want anymore," she murmurs breathlessly, gasping for air while she lies through her teeth.

Her hooded gaze locks onto mine as I hold her stare and whisper, "Are you sure about that?"

Her eyes drift shut as I ease out of her to the tip, her ass hanging in the air between us.

"You're going to beg me to come this time," I groan, meaning each and every word.

Slamming back into her, I dig my fingers into her hips as I secure her in place, pounding into her over and over, my grunts and pants mixing with the moans leaving her bloodstained lips.

"*Greyson.*" She whimpers my name, and it's nearly my undoing.

Sweat beads down my temple as I deliberately thrust into her, my balls slapping against her ass as I edge her closer to the brink of ecstasy.

She tightens around my cock, her fingernails digging into my back as I fuck her relentlessly, and I can't wait to see the marks she leaves on my skin. A piece of art.

Right as I feel her about to come, I slow down, almost coming to a complete stop. "Beg me for it, baby."

She huffs and sighs, fighting the urge to give me what I want and telling me to shut up and fuck her.

Easing out of her, I roll my hips, sinking an inch further before stopping again.

"For fuck's sake! Greyson!" She slaps my back in frustration, and I hate to admit how much I like the sting of pain.

"Did that sound like begging to you?" I ask her mockingly, my tone raspy and low as I slide a few inches deeper inside her.

Her head rolls back, and she wiggles her hips, desperate for any friction, but I hold her still. Being completely airborne isn't helping her right now. But it's sure as fuck helping me.

She cries out, "Please, please, please. *Fuck!* Please make me come. I'm so close I'm going to lose my min—"

In one swift move, I thrust into her, cutting her pleas off. I need this as badly as she does. I've been fighting my own orgasm this whole fucking time, and I'm done.

Her gasping moans bring me to the edge as I relish every pump into her, feeling her tighten around me once more. "That's it."

She rolls her neck up and meets my stare, her eyes still red as sin. She's close, and I'm right behind her.

Her gaze holds a silent question, flicking to my neck, and it takes me less than a second to answer. "Do it. Drink my fucking blood while I come in you."

Her fangs are sinking into my neck before I even finish my sentence. And we lose all control together.

She moans against me as I feel her greedily take from my veins. Her orgasm tears through her, clenching my cock as it pulses in intense waves.

Her release is my undoing.

"Oh, fuck," I whimper, crying out as I spill inside of her, coming harder than I ever have before. If I ever doubted it, I sure as hell don't now; I'm never going to get enough of her.

Walking onto campus this afternoon feels foreign, like I've never been here before. But in a way, that's kind of true, at least in terms of perspective. I'm not the same person I was when I last stepped foot here; it feels like that was a lifetime ago.

I have to turn in my laptop that I rented from the school—the last thing on my to-do list before I'm officially done with college.

The plus side of Saint Eldritch University offering classes online is that I can work ahead. I've technically been done with all of my schoolwork since before the Culling. I just had to wait for the due dates to submit everything, which I already did.

I don't know if *pride* is the right word to describe the feeling in my chest. I've completed such a big chapter of my life. But now I doubt that I'll use that degree anytime soon. I have no reason to. With the money Vivian gave me, I could go without a job for years. Although a twinge of guilt sinks into my chest for accepting the money, knowing that we are far more than vampire and bloodling now.

I might be good at math, and I respect the black-and-white way it works, but it seems so insignificant in my life right now. Look at how much of my life has changed in the last few weeks. Pursuing a career in finance sounds like the last thing I want to do.

Who knows what two months will look like from now? I certainly don't. Besides, I'm done wasting time on things that don't matter to me. I'm focusing on what I love from here on out.

Opening the door of the student affairs building, I walk straight ahead and take a right to the tech office.

"Hi, how can I help you?" the lady at the front desk greets me, and I take a sharp breath at the pain that aches in my chest.

She reminds me so much of Cheryl. God, I wish she could be here to see me graduate, to see her love and hard work pay off.

I couldn't be anywhere close to where I am without her. She was the closest thing to family I ever had, and I miss her so fucking much. Part of me kept this grief at bay, pushing through and focusing on following the dreams we built together that I didn't even allow myself the time to heal.

My eyes sting as I embrace the warm memory of the greatest woman I've ever known.

Stepping forward with a full heart, I slide the laptop across the desk. "Here to turn this back in."

She accepts it and smiles, scanning the barcode on the side and typing into her computer. "Were there any issues with it?"

"Not at all."

She stows it on the storage shelf with a hundred other devices. "Perfect. Thank you so much. You'll receive an email confirmation of the return in minutes. Have a good day."

"Thanks, you too," I respond before spinning on my heels and walking out of the room, running straight into some guy and knocking him sideways.

Holding him upright, I apologize, "Sorry, man. Are you okay?"

He nods eerily slow, staring straight ahead. His cheek twitches as he takes a step forward, but I stop him, not fully understanding why I'm doing it. But there's something so familiar about it.

He freezes, still staring soullessly ahead as I brush the overgrown brown hair from his face, sucking in a sharp breath.

Holy shit.

"Ethan?" I whisper, and his head lifts to mine, his

dead stare locking with my eyes. "Oh my god. What happened?"

No wonder I didn't recognize him right away. His tan skin has paled drastically, and his eyes are sunken into his face, dark purple and blue circles outlining them.

"Have we met?" His voice is as cold and lifeless as his movements.

"Do you not remember me?" I murmur, my stomach twisting in confusion and fear.

His eyes well with tears, but no other part of him shows emotion, his stare still stone-cold. "No, I don't know who you are."

He turns, trying to step forward, but I stop him, securing my hand around his wrist. I'm getting to the bottom of this.

His condition can't possibly be something humanly possible, and it can't be a coincidence that until this morning, he was still under the contract of the Culling.

Digging my phone out of my pocket, I call Vivian.

"Hello?" she answers on the first ring.

"Hey, how fast can you get here?" I ask her, panic laced in my voice. "Something's wrong."

I know I don't know Ethan well, but he was kind to me and seemed like a genuine guy. He definitely doesn't deserve whatever the hell happened to him. No one does.

She ends the call, the phone beeping in my ear. Stowing it back in my pocket, I know she'll be here soon, so I guide Ethan to a bench in the hallway, helping him sit down. He lets me move him any which way, like a puppet to my command. A disgusted, rage-filled chill races down my back.

The air electrifies, and the hair on the back of my neck tingles right before Vivian appears before us, crouching in front of Ethan. "What's going on? Do you know him?"

Looking at Ethan, I murmur, "I met Ethan at the Culling. He was joking and having a good time. Said he's done it for years. I barely recognized him when I bumped into him just now. It's like he's a shell of himself. Have you seen this before?"

Glancing at her, I suck in a breath. Her eyes are glazed over, like a memory is playing behind her eyes. But her face contorts from worry to anger a second later.

"You know, don't you?" I whisper. "Is he going to be okay?"

She nods, her jaw clenched tightly.

"What is it?" I study Ethan's empty gaze, wondering where his spark has gone.

She tugs at the side of his hoodie, and my

stomach churns at the image on the side of his neck. Two blackened, open wounds sink deep into his neck. Bite marks.

From the edge of the holes, jagged, bruising spider veins bulge beneath his skin, the red, black, and yellow lines disappearing beneath his hair and clothes. It almost looks like it's spreading further and further.

"What the *hell* is that?" I scoff.

"*That* is what our venom does when a human isn't willing to accept the bite and the vampire does it anyway. Whoever did this nearly drained him. I don't know how he's still walking." Rage is rolling off her in dangerous waves. "We need to find whoever did this and as fast as possible. The venom will continue to spread." Her words fall off, and I know she's holding something back from me.

"What happens if we don't find the one who did this?" I ask, demanding to know.

She meets my stare, her hazel eyes flickering with red as she struggles to control her rage. "We need the blood from whoever bite him. We have to mix it with the antidote. The venom will continue to invade his body until there's more of it than there is of him, and eventually…it will kill him."

Chapter Fourteen
vivian

Sliding his arm beneath Ethan's legs and his other arm around his back, Greyson picks him up and cradles him against his chest. "Can you grab his bag?"

Nodding, I grab Ethan's backpack from the bench and sling it over my shoulder. Thankfully, the hallway is empty as we head outside. I pull open the back passenger door, and Greyson carefully lays a very submissive Ethan into the back seat of Greyson's car.

Ethan can't help the subservient demeanor; the venom and loss of blood are the causes. But there's something different about his mind. I opened my senses to him immediately when I got there, and I didn't feel anything coming from him. Like there were no emotions at all to be felt.

Whoever did this to him tampered with his mind in some way, whether it was from an overdose of the venom or another sinister form. It's too early to know exactly what is causing this. But I will get to the bottom of this, and I will destroy the vampire that dared to do this to him.

Something catches my eye on his wrist as he settles into the seats, and I bunch his sleeve up, exposing a whole new level of horror.

The vampire didn't just bite Ethan's neck—he bit his wrists, the same disgusting venomous wounds left behind on his arms. A vampire would only do that if they wanted to inflict the most agonizing pain possible. It's cruel and sadistic on a whole new level.

My blood boils as I study Ethan, memorizing every single mark and discoloration on him, committing it to memory. No human that participates in the Culling should ever suffer like this. They volunteer as a bloodling, auctioning their blood to keep us sustained. Every vampire knows the High Council's motto: *Enough to sustain, never drain.*

"He bit him there too?" Greyson's voice is disconnected, cold, and quiet.

"Exactly what you think it is," I murmur, pulling Ethan's sleeves back down and gently shutting the car door.

"Take him to our house, and don't let anyone in," I order him.

"Where are you going?" he questions, his brows furrowed, his worry on the tip of my tongue.

Guiding him to the driver's-side door, I open it for him. "To meet with the High Council. We're going to track down the vampire responsible for this before it's too late."

I usher him inside, and he slides into the seat. Before I shut the door, I lean down, cup his face, and kiss him as deeply as I possibly can before vanishing, running to the Barlowe, crossing miles in a matter of seconds.

And I don't stop until I burst through the High Council office doors.

BOOM.

Like a bomb going off, the doors splinter apart, exploding into a million pieces as Jason jumps from his chair and takes cover.

Woah.

The doorknob falls from my hand, crashing to the pile of splintered wood. All I meant to do was grab the doorknob and open the door, not destroy the whole thing. I guess this is what Autumn was talking about when she said I'm getting stronger.

"Vivian?" Jason gasps, standing up from behind the desk. "Is that you?"

Taking heavy breaths does little to calm my erratic heart. And it has nothing to do with what just happened to the threshold of the office. "I need the records from the Culling. A boy named Ethan. Brown hair, brown eyes, maybe five foot ten inches tall. I need to know who his chosen was. And I need it *now*."

He remains frozen for a moment, processing my words before jumping into action. "Yes, of course. One second." He pauses, rapidly typing into his computer. "His chosen was Sarah Albrightson. What's going on?"

"Sarah?" I scoff. She would never have done this. "Text me her address, please. Sarah's bloodling has been nearly drained. He was forced to take the bite, and I don't know how long we have before the venom runs its course." His face pales, the same disgust and disappointment setting into his features as I feel. "I'm going to her house to see what she has to say about it. I doubt she would have done it. But you never know. Meet me there when you've called the rest of the council."

"You've got it," he states, immediately reaching for his phone.

Checking the text he sent, I look to see where her house is located. Not too far from my home. I take off running, racing out of the building, traveling faster than I ever have, feeling the power course through my veins with each step I take.

My senses are wide open when I near the house, not feeling anything coming from inside.

Knocking on the door, I wait all of two seconds before twisting the doorknob, finding it unlocked. Pushing it open, I prepare myself for anything, my shoulders stiff and reflexes sharp.

"Sarah? Are you home?" I call out, carefully stepping into the dark room, dimly lit by the sun peeking around the curtains.

No answer.

Sliding my hand up the wall, I feel the light switch and flick it on, immediately discovering exactly why Sarah didn't answer me.

Her body lies face down on the living room floor, the only exposed skin of her arms dried and shriveled, her veins now black as coal. Deadly nightshade poisoning.

If there was any doubt this was an accident, there isn't now. This was intentional. It would be damn near impossible to accidentally intake the amount needed to kill one of us. She was murdered, and her bloodling was taken.

Digging my phone out of my pocket, I call Jason, and he answers on the first ring. "We're on our way."

I fill him in on what I know so far. "She's dead. Nightshade poisoning. We'll need to take her body back to the Barlowe for now." I pause, an idea coming to mind. "I need to reach out to a friend of mine who might be able to help track down whoever did this, and then I'm going home to check on Ethan and Greyson. Keep me updated on what you guys find."

"We'll get Sarah to the hotel and see what evidence might have been left behind. Be careful. We don't know who's behind this or if they're working alone," he warns me, and I can't help but smile. I wish I would run into them—it would make this a hell of a lot easier.

Ending the call, I let myself out of the house, securing the door behind me before speeding off to my next stop, Hale Bar.

Werewolves and vampires like to keep their distance from each other. There's no rivalry like there is in the movies, no wars. At least not for a long time. Before I established the High Council and the network beneath us, vampires had a well-earned reputation for using humans like Capri Suns. Since the Culling became rooted in tradition, the relationship between werewolves and us has improved greatly since we aren't actively draining humans left and right.

Lachlan Hale is the alpha of his pack, heading the strongest and one of the largest packs in the country right out of Saint Eldritch. I've known him for a few years now. We met after a little girl in his pack went missing, allegedly abducted by a vampire.

I offered my assistance immediately, but they didn't want my help. I couldn't blame them though—I was the first one to approach them with good intentions.

He told me to stay out of it, but of course, I didn't listen. I tracked the vampire down within hours, thanks to decades of honing my hunting skills. They would have been able to find him faster had they had his scent. But they didn't know where the little girl was taken from, and they had no place to start looking.

I wasn't going to sit by and let this vampire drain this little girl. But I also wasn't going to directly piss off the local alpha either. I wanted our relationship to grow, not suffer.

Having venom antidotes readily available, all I needed was a few drops of the rogue vampire's blood to stop it from spreading in her system.

When I finally located the vampire, I used my mind-altering abilities to order him to safely bring the girl home, surrender himself to Lachlan's pack, hand over the antidote, and confess what he had done to her.

It was hard not killing him myself. But his life wasn't mine to take.

My gift works on humans and vampires. Thankfully, my encouraging words led him to bring the girl to the bar, walking straight into a room full of werewolves that dealt with him in ways that would challenge even our brutality.

Lachlan approached me days later, telling me that before they killed him, he confessed that a girl named Vivian was responsible for her safe return.

That was the beginning of our respected partnership. Every now and then, we need the abilities of one another, like our abilities required for different, unique situations. Now, I need Lachlan to help me sniff out this vampire before we run out of time.

Barely slowing down, I burst through the door of Hale Bar, thankfully not shattering it into a million pieces like I did at my hotel. Approaching the countertop, I stop right before Lachlan.

"Jesus," he gasps, jumping back like he's seen a ghost.

"I need your help." I skip the formalities of hello, getting right to the point.

He continues to casually wipe the inside of a glass. "What's going on?"

"I need you to help me track down a vampire. One that's gone rogue," I murmur, a second from grabbing the glass he's incessantly cleaning and throwing it against the wall.

"Yeah, okay. I can help after work—"

"*Now.* I need your help right now," I order him, feeling annoyance radiating from him. "Really? You're annoyed right now? *So am I.*" Grabbing his shirt, I yank him forward, smashing his ribs against the counter, the glass in his hand falling to the ground and shattering.

Every chair in the building squeaks on the floor as everyone rises to their feet, ready to protect their alpha. But I don't care if he's the big boss in charge.

"The rogue murdered one of us, kidnapped their bloodling, and nearly drained him. The venom is already pulsing through his veins. I know you know what that does to a human." I pause, feeling his annoyance shift to sympathy as he remembers the little girl, who I have since come to learn is named Gracie. "Are you willing to help me or not?" I demand, my voice booming through the room by the time I finish.

"I'll help." He exhales, raising his hands in surrender, the tiniest amount of humor lifting the corner of his lips. "Now, put your fangs away."

Shit, I didn't even realize they came out to play.

Between the intense emotions and changes my body is going through right now, I feel like I've just turned, still learning how to control my power.

Taking a shaky breath, I calm myself down, my fangs retreating into my gums as I release him from my death grip, patting the shirt over his chest, which looks permanently wrinkled.

Grabbing a napkin and a pen from the bar top, I scribble my address down and slide it to him. "Meet me here as quickly as you can. I'm heading there now."

He picks it up and nods. "I'll bring a few other members that can help."

"Thank you," I murmur, holding his stare for a moment longer to express my gratitude.

Racing out of the bar, I fly down the streets, winding left and right as I run back home.

I can't stop thinking about how easily it could have been Greyson in Ethan's place. An image of Ethan's marks on Greyson's body flashes in my mind, and I clench my fists so tightly my nails draw blood.

The thought makes me want to break every bone in the rogue's body, forcing him in a position so he never heals, and trap him in ash wood for decades, making him beg for death but never giving it.

If it had been Greyson that was targeted... I can't even finish that thought.

I have been alive for a long time, always secretly missing a piece of myself, and I didn't know how or where to find it. I didn't expect the missing piece to be a person.

The night we met and I immediately was drawn to him. The way his words found their way across the room, filling my mind. The way I haven't been able to get enough of him, his touch, his blood, his presence, everything. It all makes sense now.

Since the moment I stepped into that bar, I knew I wouldn't be able to walk away from him. At first, I was scared to even think that I could let a human into my life. I was terrified of losing someone close to me again. I didn't want to fall for Greyson, but I couldn't help it. Fate may have brought us together, but it didn't make us choose one another.

My fear of losing someone I love has kept a wedge between Greyson and my heart. But I'm tired of living that way. I'm tired of staying in the shadows. If someone dares to go after what's mine, they will pay with their lives.

The only way I can guarantee his safety is by staying right by his side, protecting him every step of the way. Which is exactly what I plan to do for a very long time.

Winding along my driveway, my legs carry me to the steps with powerful strides, leading me up to my front door.

Autumn was right about the power increase for sure. Every day, I feel stronger.

I clear my mind, readying myself for the task at hand as I open the door and step inside, immediately spotting Greyson and Ethan across the foyer in the living room, sitting on the sofa, Ethan sound asleep, snoring.

Greyson quietly rises to his feet and crosses the open space. I meet him halfway, sliding my arms around his waist and squeezing him tight.

His arms embrace me, and I breathe him in, smelling my own personal heaven.

He wheezes. "Baby, you're squeezing *really* hard."

Releasing him, I step back, an embarrassed flush spreading across my lips. "I'm sorry."

He smirks and takes a step toward me, closing the distance between us once again. "If you missed me that much, you could have just said so instead of trying to crush my ribs."

Lightly, and I mean *lightly*, I shove his chest. "I missed you. This whole thing with Ethan has me lost in my thoughts."

He tips my chin up, and that pretty baby blue stare, perfectly framed by his glasses, entrances me. "About what?"

"You. Me. Us." I take a shaky breath, sliding my fingers up his waist. "Greyson…" I take another breath for confidence. He's human, and although there are ways to grant him immortality, time is fleeting, and I don't want to hold my feelings back any longer. "I lov—"

Sporadic, wet coughing cuts me off, coming from the living room from Ethan. I speed over and suck in a sharp inhale when I discover he looks worse.

Our venom's effects work slowly through a human, prolonging their pain, and right now, we need all the time we can get. But because he's been fed on so much and mercilessly, there's so much venom in his system, speeding up the process.

"Has he talked to you at all yet?" I ask Greyson as he approaches. He shakes his head, heart-aching concern pouring off him.

"Only once, at school. I asked if he knew me, but he said he didn't. After what he's been through, I don't blame him, obviously," He sighs, sitting down by Ethan's feet.

His mind is clearly suffering more than just the bite can give. An idea flutters in my mind. Grabbing Ethan's shoulder, I lightly nudge him awake.

He opens his bloodshot eyes, silently staring straight at the ceiling.

"Help me sit him up," I tell Greyson, contemplating if what I'm about to do is a good idea.

This won't hurt him physically, but I'm nervous about messing with his mind at all if it will permanently harm him since so much damage seems to have already been done. But we don't have too much of a choice right now. We need answers.

Greyson helps without question, guiding his feet to the floor as I lift his torso, leaning him against the back of the couch.

Standing between his legs, I cup Ethan's face and take a deep breath, forcing him to look at me while releasing my power, stretching it out from my mind and latching onto his.

Forcing my question into his consciousness, I demand an answer. "Tell me who did this to you."

Ethan's voice is scratchy and raw, emotionless. "I can't."

"Why not?"

He pauses before robotically answering, "I-I don't know. But I can't tell you."

My suspicion was right—someone tampered with his consciousness, the same way I can alter other's minds. I can feel it in him, a block standing in the way of my connection to Ethan like a brick wall.

Mentally, I try to push past it, forcing my power against the block, but it doesn't budge.

Everything about my abilities has intensified thus far. Maybe it's time to test this part of it out.

Taking a steady inhale, I close my eyes, envisioning the blockage falling away, the aura of my power breaking it down.

Surging my energy through the tether, I gasp, sensing the wall beginning to come down in his mind.

Opening my eyes, I find the slightest spark igniting in Ethan's stare, the light flickering, teetering on the edge of powering on or shutting off again.

There's only one other vampire I know of that can control minds like this, other than myself.

"Ethan? Can you hear me?" Greyson pleads, his voice ragged.

Securing my grip on his mind, I command him, "Remember everything that he made you forget." Forcing my power through the cracks in his mental wall, I encourage him, "You are in control, Ethan. Remember *everything*."

As if he's pulling on the bricks from the other side, he creates an opening, large enough for my power to burst through the wall completely, shattering it apart until nothing stands between our connection.

He sucks in a sharp breath and blinks rapidly, the cloudiness in his stare fading away, his gaze locking onto Greyson's as his eyes well with tears. "G-Greyson? Is...is that you?"

Greyson throws his arms around him, and I step back, letting them embrace each other as tears flow down Ethan's face and he violently cries out. Ethan stays like that for a moment, shouting in agony as everything comes back to him.

This hasn't cured him. It only restored his memory. We are still battling the clock to get the antidote into his system. I want to give them privacy, but I also need him to confirm who his assaulter is. But I remain quiet for a little longer, giving Ethan's mind a few minutes to settle.

He's not in pain, and that only means one thing—the venom has spread far enough that it's numbed his nervous system, one of the last steps before it takes his life.

"Where am I?" Ethan asks as they pull apart, and he looks around my living room, taking everything in.

Taking a seat on the coffee table across from him, I clear my throat. "You're in my home. We brought you here after Greyson found you at the university."

Something clicks in his gaze like he recognizes me. "You're Ms. Barlowe."

Nodding, I smile. "Call me Vivian."

"Vivian. Thank you," he murmurs, his eyes

wrought with pain. His gaze falls to his hands and his wrists before he lifts the sleeve of his sweatshirt and studies the spider vein lines leading out of dark bite marks, spreading further along his skin with each passing second.

"We will find whoever did this to you. He will never be able to hurt you or anyone else ever again. I can promise you that."

His head snaps up to me. "You said *he*. You know who it is?"

Wetting my lips, my jaw ticking, I say, "I have an idea of who it might be, based on his ability to nearly wipe your mind." I take a breath. "Do you remember what he looked like? Could you describe him to me?"

His eyes slam shut, his face contorting with fear, anger, and disgust. His hands start shaking in his lap, and I hate that I have to make him go through that trauma again right now.

"H-He's older-looking. His hair is dark brown, longer, stopping at his shoulders. A couple of inches taller than me." He pauses, and I reach out and take his hands in mine, opening my senses to him. My eyes burn from the emotional agony coursing through him.

You're doing amazing. He can't hurt you anymore.

He huffs, his eyes fluttering open as his thumping

heart rate spikes. "A tattoo—he had a scorpion on the side of his neck."

It's him. *Victor Archer.*

His voice shakes, tears pooling in his eyes. "Can I ask you a question? And you promise to tell me the truth no matter what?"

"I promise," I tell him, meaning it.

His words ghost across his lips, almost too quietly to hear. "Am I going to die?"

Squeezing his hands, I shake my head. "Not if I have any say in the matter. I'm going to find him, finish the antidote, and you will be just fine."

He mouths the words *Thank you.*

Lachlan's wolfy odor invades my nose. He's here.

Speeding over to the door, I open it before he even knocks, his hand raised in the air. "Come in."

"Thank you," he grumbles, stepping inside and following me into the living room. "This is Maeve and Pierce."

"Thank you for coming. I'm Vivian," I introduce myself to them as we step into the living room. "Lachlan, Maeve, and Pierce, this is Ethan and Greyson."

"Hi," Ethan murmurs, looking up, the purple rings around his eyes still deep and dark.

"Do you smell him?" I ask Lachlan as he takes a deep breath.

He nods, pinching his nose and wincing. "Oh yeah. I couldn't miss that stench a mile away."

Hope blooms in my chest. "So you'll be able to find him?"

Lachlan's gaze shifts from Ethan to me. The chocolate brown of his eyes starts glowing the deepest shade of gold. He scoffs arrogantly, "Yeah, we'll find him."

Chapter Fifteen
greyson

Lachlan and his pack members left last night to start tracking down Victor. I know it wasn't his responsibility to help, but he did it anyway, and for that, I'm grateful.

Ethan is my friend, and I've never wished to be a vampire until that moment when his memories returned. Seeing the pure terror and agony in his eyes made me want to kill Victor myself.

I know he'll get what's coming to him; I just wish I could have a hand in it. I'm not an idiot—he could rip my heart out of my chest with one thrust of his hand and crush all of the bones in my body with ease. I don't stand a chance. But thankfully, I have

Vivian, and I think my little spitfire is ready to let some of her rage out.

She stayed back last night, wanting to keep an eye on us in case Victor came here. She didn't sleep, but it's not like she needs it. She and Lulu kept me company until I fell asleep in the living room on a sofa across the room from Ethan.

When I woke up the next morning, there was no update yet on Victor's whereabouts. The pack hunted him through the night, only stopping for a few hours of rest before continuing.

Vivian is getting ready right now to leave and join Lachlan and his pack. She said a member of the High Council will come here to take her place while she's gone, to guard outside and make sure we're safe.

"Are you sure you want to go?" I grab Vivian's waist and pull her back into me as she walks by, breathing her in.

She nods, staring down at my interlocked hands secured around her. "I have to." She takes a deep, shaky breath, and I press my lips into the top of her head. "I couldn't save Genevieve, and it haunts me every day, Grey. Ethan somehow got away, whether it was his willpower fighting through the mind hold or Victor's arrogance in releasing him. Regardless, I won't let Victor get away with it."

Spinning her in my arms, I tip her head up, sliding my fingers into her hair. "And he *won't*. You'll get him."

I want to whisk her away and hide us from the rest of the world, but we can't, and she would never let me. It's not who she is. She fights for those who need her. She refuses to allow the evils of this world to win. She's fucking incredible.

Maybe when this is all over, we can go somewhere together. Check a box off the bucket list. We just need time, for so many reasons right now. We haven't even been able to process the fact that we are bound together by fate.

I mean, what the hell does that even mean, really?

Honestly, I don't even need an explanation. Everything in my life leading up to the Culling always made me question my purpose in this world. But in truth, I think I was just waiting for her.

When this is all said and done, I'll tell her everything—how she has become the very reason I live and breathe. I was born to be by her side, destined to find her and never let her go.

She is as much a part of my being as I am, intertwined with my very soul.

I don't want her to go after him; I want to keep her safe here with me. But I know that would only hurt her. She needs this, to punish Victor for breaking the laws and to redeem herself in her mind for what happened to Genevieve.

So I let her go, but not before kissing her like it might be the last time I ever do, and when I pull away, I have no doubt in my mind that I am in love with Vivian Barlowe.

Ava arrived about four hours ago and has been keeping watch from her car outside. We haven't received word from anyone yet, which means there's nothing to report.

For the last hour, I've had a horrible feeling in my stomach, like a sense of impending doom deep in my gut. Needing a distraction, I went upstairs while Ethan was resting and cuddled with Lulu for a while before locking her in the bedroom. In case tonight gets out of hand, I want her to be safe and secure.

A few of the High Council members have volunteered to take shifts watching over us, and Jason should be here soon to take over for Ava.

Descending the stairs, I stroll to the kitchen to get a glass of water, taking a few drinks before the doorbell rings throughout the house.

Ethan nearly jumps out of his skin and pulls the blanket tighter around him on the couch as I attempt to calm him. "It's okay. It's just Jason switching out with Ava."

Walking to the front door, I peek through the peephole and see the back of Jason's head before I twist the knob and pull it open.

"Hey," I greet him. "Come in."

All the air dissipates from my lungs, and my spine chills.

Jason's knees give out, and he crumples to the ground like a doll, his arms flailing and landing in unnatural positions. As Jason's limp body falls away, a grimy man with blood dripping down the sides of his mouth steps forward, my body chilling to the bone.

"God, vampires taste gross. I could barely stomach it long enough to bite him."

My gaze falls to his blood-soaked hand, bile rising in my throat when I realize what he's holding.

A heart.

"We aren't alone," I warn him, lying through my teeth.

He smiles, and I spot the tattoo on the side of his neck, the hair on the back of my neck standing straight up.

Great.

My voice is loud enough to warn Ethan but not too loud to be obvious. "Let me guess. Victor?"

He clicks his tongue. "Indeed." He takes another step forward, and I slam the door shut, but he's too fast, blocking it with his leg. "That is not the way to treat a guest."

Fuck.

He rears his arms back, his palms facing me before he shoves my chest, and I fly ten feet in the air across the foyer, crashing painfully to the hardwood floor.

Grabbing me by my throat, he lifts me up, my toes dangling above the ground.

His eyes shift to red, and his fangs descend. "Why don't we find out what's so special about that blood of yours."

Chapter Sixteen
vivian

My patience is wearing incredibly thin as the minutes tick by and we still haven't found Victor. Lachlan and a few select members of his pack have been tracking him, even crossing state lines into Connecticut and back. They think Victor is toying with them, forcing them to run in circles while we try to catch up, two steps behind.

But finally, as we return to Saint Eldritch, Lachlan starts acting like an alpha and latches onto a stronger scent, finally leading us out of this labyrinth of a hunt.

I hear someone whisper incoherently, and I turn,

searching their faces, trying to decipher who it was, but no one is looking at me.

"*Vivian.*" I hear the voice again and immediately recognize it.

Greyson.

"Greyson?" I call out, and everyone's attention snaps my way, their eyes wide and brows furrowed.

"What is it?" Lachlan demands, walking over to me, but I don't pay him any attention, instead focusing my hearing to find Greyson's voice again.

But all I hear is the sounds of nature and Lachlan's vocalized concern.

A pit forms in my stomach, ripping my gut apart as a coldness settles into every cell in my body. "Something's wrong."

"What? What's happening?" Ava grabs my hand, begging me to answer.

I release my fangs, tapping into the power in my chest and opening all of my senses.

"Ahh!" I cry out as pain erupts in my neck.

My hand flies to it, the pain immediately fading into a strange tingling sensation, pinpointed in two perfect dots.

Oh my god.

"He's at my house. He's at my house right now. And he's…" I can't even finish the sentence. I'm already running, racing as hard and fast as I can, my feet pounding into the ground.

I'm coming. Just hold on. I'm coming.

The world around me blurs as I run with abandon, my neck burning in the two points where fangs have bitten into Greyson's neck.

Oh my god, I am going to rip the vampire to pieces.

I can't seem to move fast enough, and my chest tightens as I gasp for air. It's not for the shortness of breath but for the despair repeatedly stabbing my heart.

Tears burn in my eyes as I picture his smile in my mind. I should've listened to him when he wanted me to stay this morning. In his embrace, that's where I should be. If I had done that, this wouldn't be happening. I would have been there to protect him.

Turning onto my street, I fly down the block, tapping into the rage and uncontrollable power in my body fueling me forward. Rushing up the steps, I pause, only for a second, as I find Jason's body crumpled to the ground.

I'm so sorry, Jason.

With no time to mourn my friend, I burst through the open doors, frantically searching for Greyson, and the second I spot him out of the corner of my eye, my world shatters.

Greyson convulses on the ground as Victor holds

his head up, his blood-soaked, fanged mouth buried in Greyson's throat.

My vision turns red as something inside of me snaps, every cell in my body tearing in half and healing back together with newfound and untapped power, waves of dark red energy radiating from me.

I blink and reach them, digging my fingers into the flesh of Victor's neck.

"Get off of him!" I roar, my voice tearing through the house like an earthquake.

I don't want to rip him off if I don't have to. The pain of the fangs coming out against their will would be excruciating for Greyson.

Victor laughs, and I see the venom dancing beneath Grey's paling skin, spidering out from Victor's mouth.

Greyson's blood runs down Victor's chin and neck, soaking into his shirt. Sinking my fingertips an inch into his flesh, I secure him in my grip.

"This is going to hurt, Greyson. And I'm so sorry," I warn him before lifting up on Victor's head, holding him in place as I slide my other hand into his mouth, pressing down on his tongue.

As easily as I snap a twig in half, I push down, a deafening, wet pop bursting in the air as I snap his jaw in half.

He growls in pain, releasing Greyson and falling backward, my fingers still buried in his neck.

His arms flail around him as he tries to break free of my grasp, and all I can do is laugh and smile at him because he has no idea what's coming to him. Excruciating agony is all he will ever know from this moment forward. He will beg me for mercy, and I will never grant it.

Fisting his shirt in my hands, I lift him from the ground and toss him across the room like a stuffed animal. He explodes through the wall, tearing straight through the Sheetrock and every layer until he bursts through the brick on the outside of the house.

I speed outside, catching him by the throat before he even has a chance to land and run.

My vision pulses red as anger overwhelms me, surrounding me completely as I grab him by his leg with one hand and his throat with the other. In one swift movement, I lift him up and slam him down, thrusting my knee upward. A bone-curdling crunch snaps through the air as I drive my knee through his break, snapping it in half.

The best part about torturing a vampire is that they'll heal up just as strong as before. I can break his spine over and over, and he'll heal every single time, feeling the pain just as intensely as the first time.

Rage and an animalistic desire to break every

single bone in Victor's body courses through my veins. Throwing him over my shoulder like a towel, I look up, bend my knees, and push off the ground.

As if gravity struggles to control me, I fly up onto the roof, Victor slung over my back. Grabbing his ankle, I whip him off me, slamming him against the black shingles.

He stares up at me, his jaw dangling from his face. It has to be set properly before it will start to heal. Which means until then, he feels every second of pain.

Grabbing him by the waist, I raise him up over my head, his weight as light as a feather above my arms. Facing the edge of the roof, my eyes lock onto the black fountain.

Digging my feet into the ground, I take a few running steps before pushing off the roof, soaring through the air toward the large fountain.

He had the audacity to bite Greyson. To break into my home and hurt the one I love. He wanted to challenge me, and this will be his outcome. He deserves an eternity in agony, and that is exactly what I will grant him.

As we descend through the cold night air, I tighten my grip and swing his body down hard on top of the decorative point. The black marble bursts through his chest, blood exploding into the air like a water feature, spraying me in drops of his insides as I skewer him on the post, forcing him down to the hilt. He screams out in agony, and I bathe in the sounds of his horror.

Grabbing his hair, I turn his head, forcing him to look at me, my words a spitting growl. "You never should have touched him." Grabbing his other hand with mine, I snap his index finger and twist, ripping the flesh apart at the knuckle. "When you lie entombed in your coffin with nightshade filling your every breath and you question what got you there, I want you to remember this moment. That *I'm* the reason you will writhe in pain for all of eternity. *I'm* the reason Death will never greet you and bring you peace, and I'm the reason Mercy will *never* offer you a helping hand."

Lachlan rushes over to me, jumping up the edges of the fountain, his face twisting in horror. "Go to him. We've got Victor."

Greyson needs me, as does Ethan. I can keep punishing Victor later. But in the meantime, I need to finish and add the final ingredient—Victor's blood.

"Vivian." Greyson's distant whisper tears my attention from the bloody mess before me.

"Don't you dare kill him. He's not done paying for his sins."

Lachlan nods, and I kick off the fountain and

race inside, heading straight for Greyson, passing the other wolves. I can feel his heartbeat pound into my ears and the connection between us pulsing strongly, a gravity of its own pulling us to one another.

The sight of him lying on the ground rips my heart out of my chest. He's holding his throat, writhing in pain, and it makes me want to turn around and break Victor's back all over again. But I don't. I have forever to torture Victor. Right now, Greyson needs me.

Grabbing the box of antidote mixes I keep stashed in the coffee table in my living room, I race over to Greyson, tears welling in my eyes. My anger fades to the background, and pure, gut-wrenching fear overwhelms my body.

"It's okay, baby. I'm right here. Everything's going to be okay." His eyes bulge from his head as he tries to catch his breath, his hands wrapped tightly around his throat.

"Vivian! What can I do?" Autumn calls out, dropping to her knees beside me.

Setting the vials down, I pop the cork off the top, hold Victor's severed finger over it, and squeeze drops of his blood, finishing the potion.

"Mix the other one and get it to Ethan," I order her, and she jumps into action, taking Victor's finger from me and running to find Ethan.

Caressing Greyson's jaw, I tip his head back, his mouth falling open, and I press the glass vial against his lips before pouring it into his mouth.

"Swallow it," I murmur to him, my chest erupting in pain as I watch the agony warp his features.

He gulps it down, and I wait for the relief to kick in, but nothing happens. I wait another five seconds, but again, nothing changes.

"Stop, make it stop. Why isn't it working?" I cry out, my words heaving with my desperate gasps as I cry out for help. "Autumn! Autumn!"

I can feel her presence, sense her emotions inside of the house.

My scream builds deep in my lungs, and I release it like a weapon. "Autumn!"

The ground shakes beneath us, the paintings and chandelier rattling with intense power as my cry rips through the house.

My head whips to the side as Autumn rushes over, heading straight for us.

Fear strikes her core as she meets my eyes, faltering her step slightly before she pushes it away and focuses on Greyson. "W-What's happening?"

"It's not working. Why isn't it working?!" I beg her for an answer.

She examines him as he groans and whimpers in pain, the anger boiling back up inside of me.

Her voice is shaky and ragged. "The antidote will work, but only once the venom finishes spreading through his entire body."

"We can't leave him like this! Do something!" I snap at her.

Tears well in his eyes as Autumn stutters, "I c-can't. We have to wait for the venom to run its course in his system. But the second it does, the antidote will heal him. Y-You know that."

Turning back to Greyson, I stroke his cheeks. His eyes lock with mine before slamming shut, his face twisting, tears rolling down his face.

"Make it stop, please. *Make it stop*," I sob.

Hope blossoms in my chest, and it takes me a second to realize the feeling isn't my own. It's Autumn's emotion.

"Say it. What are you thinking? What can I do?" I beg her, not turning away from Greyson.

Sadness and fear sink into her chest. "There's something else, but I don't even know if it will work. You're better off leaving things be."

I warn her, "Autumn, I like you. But please, *don't* make me ask again."

Her eyes bulge as she sees it, feeling shocked and surprised. "I've never seen it done, okay?" She pauses, and I glare at her. "You have to get the venom out of his system. But I don't know if it will even take his pain or if it will work at all. But it will certainly infect you as if Victor bit you himself. And then you're in the same position as Greyson, suffering until the venom runs its course. We'll have to get another antidote. It's too risky, Vivian. You should wait."

My mind is already made up. "Go. If you don't want to watch, then leave. Or go grab another antidote bottle from the living room and mix it with Victor's blood because I'm going to need it. I'm not going to sit here and let him suffer!"

I can't. I can't just sit here and watch this. If there's a chance I can take his pain away, I'm going to try. I don't care if it hurts me—I'll do it a thousand times over for him. But it doesn't matter what warning she gives me…my decision is already made.

Tears fall down my face, splashing onto his torn and tattered shirt. "It'll be okay, Grey. I'll make it all better."

There's only one fast way to get the venom out of his system.

Gently peeling his hands away, I give him no time to protest before I latch onto his neck, sinking my fangs into the same puncture wounds that Victor left behind.

Vampire venom is not all the same; we each create our own unique strain, only being immune to the venom our own bodies produce.

My insides burst into flames the second Victor's venom hits my tongue. It feels like I drank a gallon of gasoline and swallowed a lit match. But I don't stop. I suck hard, taking every drop of it from Greyson's veins.

As long as I can get it all out, he'll be okay. He has to be okay.

My hands start shaking as I cradle his head and grip his shoulder, holding on for dear life. I can take this pain if it means he doesn't have to. I can stomach it. I repeat it like a mantra. I have to do this.

My brain pounds against my skull, trying to shatter it into a million pieces while the sensation of a thousand knives slices into my body.

Swallowing hard, I force myself to keep going even though everything inside of me is begging me to stop. But looking at Greyson's blond hair and holding his limp shoulder gives me all of the strength I need to carry on.

I won't fail him like I failed Genevieve. I didn't have the chance to save her. She was drained dry, and I know if I hadn't gotten here in time, Victor would have drained Greyson too.

Time becomes a blur as I swallow the venom, drop after drop. My mind begins to melt, and my confidence begins to waver.

But the second Greyson's blood hits my tongue, I

know I've done it. His bloodstream is clear; his body is clear. He relaxes in my grip, every stiff muscle melting to the ground. I release my fangs and sit up, sliding my hands along Greyson's jaw.

His eyes are more alert, livelier, his stare telling me everything he wants to say without speaking a single word. I smile back at him, tears continuing to flow down my cheeks as the pain becomes overwhelming, stars bursting in my eyes. Resting my head on Greyson's chest, I know that if they can't get the antidote to me in time and this is what kills me, I will die in my happiest place in the world, in Greyson's arms.

The pain begins to fade, but I don't know if that is my body beating the side effects or the venom paralyzing me.

"Vivian, hold on!" Autumn yells from somewhere in the house.

She'll do it. She'll mix the antidote in time. She'll save me.

When a human is bitten, the venom works slowly through their system. Depending on the amount injected, the side effects will activate slower or faster. But the inevitable outcome is the same.

Because a vampire's metabolism is so quick, the effects hit us twenty times faster.

Ava announces to anyone listening, "Ethan is

doing better. The antidote is already working on him!"

Skylar runs over, coming from who knows where, and gasps when she sees me. "Oh my god, Vivian. What can I do?"

Enough worrying about me. They need to make sure Greyson is okay.

"Take care of him," I order her, but she stays still.

Autumn's brows furrow as she desperately tries to understand me. "*Tool cup oh fast?* I don't get it."

What? That is not what I said at all.

It's the venom—it's hitting my nervous system and fucking with my speech.

I hold her stare before nodding and flicking my gaze at Greyson, using the only part of me I seem to still be able to use.

"I've got him, don't worry," Ava assures me before gently sliding Greyson out from beneath my head and picking him up. "Autumn, where should I take him?"

Autumn rushes over to my side, a look of determination on her face. "Take him upstairs. He needs to rest. I'll check on him in a minute."

As Greyson is carried away from me, the sound of his whisper roars into my ears, bringing me back to life just enough to hold on. "*Vivian.*"

I want to tell him, *I'm right here and it's okay.* But I

know my body isn't functioning right. I need to take this one step at a time. Taking a deep breath, I steady my racing heart, just trying to survive.

They will take care of him. He'll be okay now.

Ava rushes over, crouching down beside Autumn.

Autumn takes charge, her voice commanding but strained. "We need to flip her over. Get her mouth open."

My body is limp and lifeless as they roll me over and part my lips. My mind feels fuzzy, and I feel light, like I'm floating in the air.

A disgusting metallic liquid hits my tongue as she tips the vial into my mouth. Mustering all of the energy I have left, I swallow the antidote. Let's just hope there's still time.

Autumn's heavy breathing fills my ears as she wraps her arms around me and squeezes me tight. "It has to work, Vivian. It has to." She rocks me back and forth, rubbing my back before pulling away.

"What do we do now?" Ava asks, panic still shaking her voice.

"Take her up to her bed. All we can do is wait and hope that we got it to her in time." Autumn wipes the tears from her cheeks as Ava scoops me into her arms.

The ceiling above me blurs for seconds as Ava

hyper-speeds me to my bedroom, carefully laying me down on the bed.

Pressure digs into my chest, and I quickly realize it's Lucy. She nestles her head into the crook of my neck. *My sweet girl.*

Autumn rushes into the room, not stopping until she reaches my side and grabs my hand. "Greyson and Ethan are resting in separate rooms. They'll be just fine, Vivian. You did it. You saved them."

Her words become soft and muffled, and I wonder why she's covering her mouth or why I can't see her face as silence trickles into my ears, her voice cutting in and out.

Why can't I hear her? Why can't I see anything, for that matter?

My thoughts are beginning to scramble, and everything around me falls eerily quiet as my mind falls victim to the venom.

Chapter Seventeen
vivian

My eyes fly open, and I gasp for air.

Where's Greyson?

"Woah, take a breath." Ava's sweet voice calms me as her hands pin me to the bed. "You're okay."

Sitting up, I clear my throat. "Where's Greyson?"

"He's in the other room. He hasn't woken up yet, but he's doing just fine. Autumn gave him a mild sedative to keep him calm and a few healing potions to help. He's a bit dinged up from fighting with Victor. But he'll wake up soon. For now, you need to rest."

My chest heaves as I suck in lungfuls of air, my

heart thumping in my ears. *Why is everything so loud right now?*

Her shoe drags across the floor, and I can hear a tiny pebble stuck beneath her shoe, sounding like nails on a chalkboard.

"Take a deep breath," Ava instructs me, and I listen.

Flattening my palms on my thighs, I close my eyes and take a slow and steady breath, holding it for a few seconds before gradually exhaling.

Images of what happened flash in my mind. Victor biting Greyson. Me breaking Victor's jaw. Ugh, the gory image churns my stomach. But I would do it again, hell I just might when I see him.

I can't believe all of that happened. I don't know what came over me; I just know I wanted to inflict the most pain on him.

"There you go," Ava says softly as the memory of everything floods my brain.

And then, an image that stalls my heartbeat flashes. The red energy wave pulsing off me. *What the hell was that?*

I have too many questions. But first, I need to see Greyson. Blinking away the fog, I look around the room and quickly recognize it. It's my bedroom. But it feels a hell of a lot emptier without Greyson.

"Your eyes changed," Ava murmurs, drawing my attention back to her.

"W-What do you mean?" I ask. "They're not hazel anymore?"

She chuckles. "Your human eyes are still hazel, yes. And your vampire ones are still red, but…hold on. I'll just let you see for yourself." She walks into my en suite and returns a moment later with a mirror, handing it to me when she sits back down in the chair beside my bed.

Holding it up, I stare at my reflection, my human appearance showing in full. My black hair is a curly mess that desperately needs to be brushed, and my sun-kissed skin could use a little lotion. But I look relatively normal.

Ava studies me intently as I glance at her and back at the mirror, taking a shaky breath and releasing my fangs and feeling the power spread throughout my body. Opening my eyes, I suck in a sharp breath.

Woah. That is new.

My hazel eyes transform into the same dark shade of red they usually do, but trickling outward beneath my eyes are translucent red spider veins.

"When were you going to tell me that you and Greyson were *lamia et fatis sanguis*? *Hmm*? Did you just feel like keeping that mind-blowing secret to yourself?" she asks, pursing her lips together.

Dropping the mirror to the bed, I press my tongue into my cheek. "Look, there was no time between us even discovering it ourselves and this chaotic shitstorm that happened. I planned on telling all of you once I could actually process it myself. Understand it. It still feels like a dream. There's still so much we don't know."

"Do you know how incredible it is? We believed it to be a myth, a story that we read about growing up. Even humans love the story of the fated vampire and bloodling. And here you are, the legend personified. It's incredible, Vivian." She exhales, her eyes wide with wonder and amazement.

"Well, try to keep it under wraps for now. We don't need anyone targeting us while we heal." I grin.

"Does it feel different? Do you feel tied to him in some way? What's it like?" She fires questions at me before sealing her lips shut, zipping them with her thumb and forefinger and tossing the key away. "Sorry, I know you just woke up," she apologizes, holding her hands up, and I laugh.

"It's okay, really. It's a nice distraction while I wait for Greyson to wake."

Her gaze flicks away from mine before returning,

and I swear I can see a question on the tip of her tongue. "Have you thought about completing the Ceremony of *Vita et Mors* with him?"

Secretly every single day since we've met.

"Yes. Countless times," I admit, my heart feeling like it's close to exploding from how hard it's pounding in my chest.

She beams as the words race past her lips. "I think you should. It's obvious you're meant for each other. And it would just keep him safer in the long run."

"Yeah…" I trail off.

I know she's right. I want to bond with him more than anything. But it's the biggest commitment a human can possibly make. Human marriage is nothing in comparison to this bond.

The Ceremony of *Vita et Mors*, or the Ceremony of Life and Death, is performed by a powerful witch. It's the act of a vampire and a human merging their souls into one. It grants the human immortality, tying their life to their vampire. But if one of them dies, so does the other. The ceremony ties them together in both life and death. There's no going back once it's done. If the ceremony is performed, it's permanent.

I want that, I know I do. I want Greyson today, tomorrow, forever. If it would be possible, I would go back in time and find him sooner so I could have him as part of my past too.

I know Greyson has feelings for me, but that kind of commitment is not one to take lightly. I've been around a lot longer than he has. How can I ask him to make that kind of decision? What if he wakes up and regrets it in ten years?

"Vivian?" Greyson's raspy voice sounds in the hallway, pulling me from my thoughts.

Ripping the covers off me, I throw myself off of the bed. My feet pound on the heated hardwood floor, carrying me toward him as he steps into the room, my eyes welling up at the sight of him.

"Oh, *thank god*," he cries out, closing the distance between us and pulling me into his embrace, instantly picking me up and securing me around his bare waist.

Overwhelming emotion bubbles out of me, and I uncontrollably heave and sob as he caresses my head, holding me tightly against his chest.

His fear emanates off him, but not the kind of fear you have when you're scared for your life but when you're scared for someone else's.

Tears stream down my face as I pull back and slide my hands along his jaw. "I'm so glad you're okay. I don't know what I would have done if…"

"Shhh. It's okay, baby. I'm right here," he

murmurs, his eyes red and wet with emotion. "I'm right here. And I'm not going anywhere."

Greyson carries us further into our room, turning around and sitting on the bed with me still wrapped around him. It is only in his arms that I am able to be weak, to be vulnerable and raw. Is that what love is? Finding strength in the embrace of another?

"I'll give you guys some privacy," Ava whispers before dismissing herself from the room, shutting the door behind her.

Our breathing syncs up, slowly calming down while we hold each other, just listening to the thump of our hearts.

"I was so scared…when I felt that poke in my neck as he bit you…I lost it." I hold his stare through his glasses, the blues of his eyes brighter than ever. "I'm so sorry I wasn't able to protect you."

My gaze staggers to his chest, but he lifts it back up, wrapping his hand around the back of my head, threading his fingers into my messy hair. "Are you kidding me?"

"W-What?" I stutter.

"Vivian, you saved my life. You *did* protect me. You got him off of me. You sucked the venom from my throat, even when it was killing you. You are the only reason I'm breathing right now." His words are heated, burning with passion. "*Fuck*, Vivian. You are the *reason* I breathe, the reason I exist." He sucks in a breath, his chest rising and falling rapidly, his eyes softening with every word. "Vivian, I love you."

My heart stops in my chest. "You do?" I whisper, my voice barely audible.

He leans forward, his lips mere inches from mine. "You have no idea how much I love you. There isn't a single thing in this world that I wouldn't do for you. You became my life the moment you walked into it."

All the air leaves my lungs, every beat of my heart pounding in my ears. Nothing

I lash out, grabbing the back of his neck and pulling him forward, claiming his lips and kissing him deeply, sweeping my tongue into his mouth as I rock against him. Rolling my forehead against his, I murmur into his parted, panting lips, "I love you too."

He grins from ear to ear as he pulls away, his cheeks turning a deep red. "Good. Because you're stuck with me."

"Forever?" I purse my lips, eyeing him playfully.

He leans forward and presses a gentle kiss against my forehead. "Forever."

The thump of his heartbeat and the flow of blood racing through his veins fill my ears, sounds I never knew I could love so much.

His brows furrow as he asks, "About that...how does that work since, you know, I'm not a vampire?"

The fact that he wants to be with me for life means the world to me. "There is no pressure to give me forever. If you want to stay mortal and live your human life, I will happily take every year you have."

His hands fall to my waist, his thumbs brushing back and forth. "And if I want to have forever with you?"

Sliding off his lap, I hold his stare. "Then there's a way to do it."

"Are you going to make me earn every word, or will you just tell me?" he asks, his gaze darkening as it drops to the opening of my pajama top.

"I mean, I like the idea of you earning the answer," I chuckle. "I don't want to freak you out."

His head tips back as he cackles. "You know that sounds crazy, right? I unknowingly participated in an auction where vampires bid on me. I moved in with one and let her feed on me whenever she desired. I was attacked by a vampire, and one of my friends was nearly killed. I promise you, nothing could freak me out, Vivian."

Swallowing hard, tears pool in my eyes at his words. "If you say so," I tease, my nerves eating me alive. "It's a ceremony called *Vita et Mors*. It would bind your soul to mine and link us eternally. Hypothetically, when we would merge our souls…you would become immortal." I hesitate, worried that I'm going to scare him away. But he hasn't run yet, and as I sense his feelings, all I find is…love and admiration with a hint of intrigue. "But there's no going back once the ceremony is completed. No magical undo button. We would be tied to one another for eternity. Destined to live and die together."

"How do we do it?" he asks casually, as if he is asking how to order takeout.

Resting my hands on his chest between us, I smile. "There's no rush. We can do it anytime or never. The choice is completely up to you."

He huffs, a cocky smirk lifting his lips.

"What?" I ask, my heart sinking.

His blue eyes burn into mine so intensely that I'm afraid I might burst into flames. "Viv, there is no doubt in my mind that I want to spend it with you. Forever and a fucking day. I'm yours, always."

He hands me his heart in his hands and seals his promise with a kiss.

KNOCK KNOCK.

Sensing who it is, I feel Autumn's essence, and she's lucky I like her, or I would have put my fist through her chest. "Come in."

I move to sit beside Greyson, and he slides his

hand in mine as Autumn walks in, the biggest smile on her face.

"I'm so happy to see you both are awake and well." Autumn's voice is smooth and calm as she takes a seat in the lounge chair across from us. "We should probably talk," she says, and panic sinks into my chest.

"About what?" I ask, my stomach twisting with concern.

"I need to tell you the truth about *lamia et fatis sanguis*. The story you and the rest of the world know is only half of the truth."

My stomach falls to the floor, waiting for the shoe to drop.

"W-What do you mean?" My voice is a ghost on my lips.

The first line she mutters blows my mind. "*The Book of Destiny* wasn't written by a vampire. The story was created to inspire love and fate. But it was written by the most powerful witch, the first witch, actually. Cordelia Hutchins." She smiles mischievously. "It's not only vampires that have their secrets."

"Wait, *what?*" I ask, confused more than anything. "Why would we have a different version of the story?"

"Your version is the one that everyone knows. The one created as a fable, a story to entertain the reader. To give them hope of finding true love and power." She takes a breath before continuing. "Cordelia was the most powerful witch of all time, gifted with the ability to see the past and the future. The story as you know it was created with bits and pieces of the truth, but her real and honest written word was hidden and protected by generations of witches, never to be revealed until the story came to life."

"And it finally did," I murmur, finishing her train of thought.

"Exactly. I certainly never expected it to happen to a friend of mine, if it even happened in my lifetime at all. You see, this spell was cast centuries ago."

"A spell?" I interrupt. "I thought it was a prediction?"

She glares at me for interrupting, and I seal my lips shut, letting her finish. "She cast a spell that floated through time and space, capable of latching on to two people at any given moment."

Glancing at Greyson, I find him listening intently, his eyes full of wonder.

Autumn continues. "But these two souls, a human and a vampire, would only be gifted power by the spell if they were truly meant to be together. Not because some witch said so, but because this fated couple endured endless pain, suffering, and heartbreak that would challenge the good in their hearts…"

Greyson has experienced lifetimes of tribulations during his short time on Earth, yet he's one of the most genuine people I've ever met. He chooses to see the good when the world is constantly trying to show him the bad.

"But despite all of that agony, they still found one another anyway. Fate is fickle. You two may be soulmates. But it's not black-and-white." I hang on to everything she says. "If either of you would have made a different step at any point in your lives and never met in that bar, the spell would have continued to search for a home for eternity."

Chills erupt down my arms at her words. The mere chances of this happening at *this* point in time with me and Greyson is so unimaginable I almost can't fathom it.

"If your choices took you down different paths, you still may have found love. You could have been happy with someone else, but a part of your heart would have never stopped searching for one another, yearning for more. You can ignore fate, but sometimes fate doesn't ignore you. When you touched that night you met, your souls became intertwined, and the spell has been activating inside of both of you since then."

"In both of us?" Greyson asks, sitting up taller.

Autumn nods. "Yes, if the spell hasn't manifested yet, you wouldn't have noticed. But you'll get stronger and faster, your strength rivaling that of vampires."

"Woah." Greyson exhales. "That'll be...*interesting*."

My heart skips a beat at the thought of him gaining those abilities.

The question flows from my lips without thought. "If we complete the Ceremony of *Vita et Mors*, will that enhance even more?"

Her eyes light up, and I swear I hear a tiny squeal slip past her lips. "First off, *yes*, I would be honored to perform the ceremony for you two. And secondly, the Ceremony of Life and Death will grant him immortality that the spell will not. It may enhance his strength even more, but to be honest, I'm not sure either way. There's no book for this."

My cheeks burn at her enthusiasm for the ceremony, and I chuckle nervously. "We haven't said for sure if we're doing the ceremony or no—"

Greyson cuts me off, his warm tone sending enticing shivers up my back as his intense stares locks on mine. "Did I not make myself clear enough earlier? I want to do it."

My heart skips a beat. "Are you sure?" Greyson, this is a huge decision."

"Are you not?" he challenges me, a playful gleam in his gaze.

Grinning, I answer honestly, "I'm *very* sure. I just don't want you to feel pressured into it."

He grabs my hand, taking it in his. "I love you, Vivian. I meant it the first time I said it, and I mean it now. I've never told anyone that—I don't take it lightly. I want to do it. I want forever with you."

"Then it's settled," I murmur, my heart feeling like it's going to burst in my chest, Greyson's love warming my entire body.

Beaming from ear to ear, he turns to Autumn. "What do you need?"

Giddiness and glee take over her emotions. "You two. A full moon. And a dagger."

Chapter Eighteen
vivian

It's been three weeks since Victor attacked our home, murdering Jason and attempting to kill Ethan and Greyson.

The members of the High Council held Victor for me, keeping him tucked away until I was ready to deal with him. Which was the first item on my to-do list when I returned. I took extreme care in crafting his coffin, which has since been sealed in concrete, deep in the depths of the Barlowe. I meant what I said to Victor that night. I meant *every* word.

He will pay not only for what he did to Ethan and Greyson but for taking the life of one of my dearest friends, Jason Belmoore. We honored his life the way vampires do, burning his body and setting the ash free to find peace, wherever that may be.

Our worst nightmare is being trapped in a coffin, especially in death, because our soul will remain trapped in our body unless set free by fire.

The High Council and everyone who was there the night of Victor's attack attended his memorial, celebrating his life both as a human and as a vampire.

Jason will be missed, but he will be remembered forever, his picture hanging in the hall of the Barlowe for everyone to see. I hate that his life was cut short by that monster, and I can't help but feel some of the blame for his death. But I will honor his life every day, upholding his respect for the High Council and the success of the Culling.

Victor's attack feels like so long ago somehow; so much has happened in the last few weeks. Greyson and I agreed to complete the Ceremony of Life and Death. He has officially graduated from college and completely made himself at home, turning the entire basement into his own personal library.

Lucy, who he insists loves his nickname for her—Lulu—has become a Velcro kitty, never far from her favorite person in the world—who is definitely *not* me. Which I find incredibly offensive since I've known her far longer and love her unconditionally, spoiling the hell out of her for years. But I also can't blame her. Greyson's my favorite person too.

We stayed in a happy bubble at our house for a couple of days before I needed to return to the High Council, even though they insisted on me taking all of the time I needed…

KNOCK. KNOCK. KNOCK.

Greyson knocks on the bedroom door, pulling me from my thoughts, my heart nearly jumps out of my mouth. "Hey, slowpoke. We're ready for you."

Slowpoke. Yeah, right. I laugh as I step into my favorite pair of black heels, the same ones I wore the night of the Culling, and the perfect complement to the red satin gown that flows over my body, accentuating every curve.

A thigh-high slit runs up my right leg, parting as I step toward the door with my heart in my throat. I spent way too long putting my hair in a curly updo, a few curls hanging loose and framing my face. But I wanted to look perfect. After all, this is the most important night of my life.

Wrapping my fingers around the doorknob, I take a shaky breath, the resident bats in my stomach flying around like crazy.

This is it, the moment the last three weeks of waiting have been leading up to, the moment my *entire life* has been leading to.

Pulling the door open, I take yet another deep breath, but there's no point because the second my gaze locks onto the white button-up on Greyson's chest, all the air in my lungs dissipates.

His smooth voice wraps around me, pulling me closer to him. "Forever? I get to stare at you for *eternity*? How did I get so damn lucky?"

My cheeks burn as I lift my gaze, meeting his eyes. "You may get sick of me eventually. It could happen."

He offers me his hand, which I happily take. "I quite literally could never tire of you."

Guiding me into the hallway, he lifts my hand, spinning me beneath his arm, bubbling laughter spilling out of me as he twirls me around, and I can't help but be reminded of how much I love this man.

His voice deepens, a raspiness there that wasn't before. "You look...beautiful, Vivian."

If my cheeks were warm before, they are ablaze right now. "Thank you."

He leads me toward the staircase, stopping me right before I try to take my first step. "Allow me."

My brows furrow as I turn to him, the sweetest smile lifting his full lips. Scooping me up into his arms, he places a gentle kiss on my forehead, curling me into his chest. He holds my stare, the warm light of the giant chandelier reflecting off his glasses.

"Life with you feels like a dream, Vivian. And I never want to wake up," he murmurs, his soft voice caressing my heart as he slowly and carefully descends the stairs with ease.

As his feet hit the floor of the foyer, I wiggle to get down, but he only squeezes me harder with a cocky smirk, refusing to let me down until we are in front of the double front doors.

"Last chance to back out," he whispers into my ear as he lowers me to my feet.

Turning in his arms, I look straight up at him, fixing the collar of his shirt. "I think I should be the one saying that to you."

"If there are no objections—" He pauses, stepping beside me as we both face toward the doors. "—then we better get started." His voice gets louder, projecting his next words, which are definitely not intended for me. "We're ready."

"What?" I ask, confused, but my question is quickly answered.

The doors pull open simultaneously, and my jaw falls to the floor as I take in the most romantic scene. A white aisle lies before us, lined by hundreds of burning candles, casting the softest glow on everything around us.

Tears well in my eyes as I take in every detail. Endless red, white, and gold-painted flowers surround the path, growing taller and fuller further down the aisle. I can't help noticing the absence of roses in the space. *He remembered.*

At the very end of the path stands Autumn, centered in front of the giant black fountain, the sounds of the flowing water like music to my ears.

Greyson clears his throat, and I turn to him, in awe of the man that stands before me. His blond hair is grown out slightly and parted down the center, tousled atop his head, not a strand out of place. He's perfect, every inch of him.

Those pretty blue eyes shine with love as his next words brand themselves in my memory. "You never belonged in the shadows, Vivian. You deserve to shine in the light."

Autumn holds the doors open with her magic as we descend down the first step toward forever. With every stride forward, my heart thumps in my chest, even more so when Greyson's hand dances along my wrist, his fingers intertwining with mine.

Greyson has granted me a gift more powerful than I've ever wielded. He's seen my darkest parts, the broken and jaded pieces I'm not always proud of, and he chooses me anyway. He makes me feel loved like I've never experienced and cherished like I never knew possible.

Before Greyson, I hid from all of those things,

deep in the depths of the darkest shadows, only emerging for my two outings a year the night before the Cullings, the Cullings themselves, and the needs of the High Council.

It was him that brought me back to life, him that made me open up and rid myself of the fear that ruled my decisions for so long.

If I had never met him, I still would have survived, serving the High Council with honor and grace, protecting those who need me most.

But a dream I've long forgotten about was brought back to life when I met him. The possibility of finding the love that I've yearned for since I was a little girl who first heard the story of the *lamia et fatis sanguis*.

There is nothing wrong with dreaming of a fairy-tale romance. There is nothing wrong with craving love more than power. I waited lifetimes for this moment, and now that I know what it's like to be loved by him, I don't want to ever remember what it's like to live without him.

Tears fall from my lashes as I stare into the eyes of the man who I've been searching for my entire life.

"Are you okay?" he leans down and whispers into my ear, pressing a gentle kiss on my cheek.

"More than you will ever know."

His eyes soften, his eyebrows pinching together. "Are you sure?"

Biting down on my bottom lip, I take a big stride forward, dragging him along with me, a smile stretching across his face, ear to ear. "I've never been more sure. Now, hurry up. I can't wait any longer. I have already waited almost two hundred years for you. I'm not waiting another second."

He rushes forward, tugging my hand, and I giggle as I match his pace, racing toward Autumn.

We come to a halt in front of her, and she welcomes us with the biggest grin and overwhelming joy. "Greyson. Vivian. It is my absolute honor to bind you two together beneath this full moon tonight."

My body is vibrating from adrenaline and anticipation. Greyson's thumb swipes across the back of my hand, and I take a deep, steady breath, calming my erratic heart.

Autumn's gaze bounces back and forth between us. "The ceremony is rather short but permanently binding. To start, I need a few drops of blood from you both." She turns, grabbing a wrapped blade from the edge of the fountain. "Vivian. You will go first."

She hands me the blade and grabs a gold chalice that is already nearly full to the brim, the liquid a stunning lavender color with herbs and flower petals floating on the surface.

Taking the knife, I raise my hands above the mixture and draw it across my palm, tilting my hand to allow the blood to drip into the cup.

"Perfect. Now you, Greyson," she instructs, and I carefully hand him the blade.

Calmly, he cuts his hand in the same way I did, the blood dripping into the chalice. A bubble emerges from the bottom, and as it floats to the surface, the color changes to a deep maroon.

Autumn takes the blade from Greyson before handing him the cup. "Wonderful. Each of you needs to take a drink from it and then hold both hands in front of you, facing each other."

He holds my stare, raising the chalice to his lips before taking a drink and swallowing. "Mmm. Delicious."

"Is it?" I chortle, accepting it from him.

He purses his lips and shakes his head like he just sucked on a lemon, and I can't help the laugh that bubbles out of me, earning an award-winning smile from him.

Lifting the cup to my lips, I take a mouthful of the tart, musty, and floral-tasting potion, swallowing it with ease, knowing that this is the next step in granting me forever with Greyson.

After handing it back to Autumn, she sets it back on the fountain. Greyson turns, taking my hands in his, and a shock runs through me from his touch.

She rests a hand on each of our shoulders that are closest to her. "A reminder to you both that you must say it with true intention, or the spell won't work." She pauses briefly, turning her attention to Greyson. "Greyson, look her in her eyes and repeat after me... I vow my life."

His stare burns into mine as he recites the words. "I vow my life."

Autumn feeds him the next line. "I vow my forever."

He repeats each word with passionate emphasis. "I vow my forever."

Autumn continues. "I vow my soul."

He wet his lips before saying, "I vow my soul."

She gives him the last line, and he repeats it, lightly squeezing my hands. "I bind myself to Vivian Barlowe from this night forward, for all of eternity."

Something stirs deep in my chest, like a door appearing that wasn't there before.

"Beautiful. Perfectly done. Now, Vivian, we'll move to you," she says, the moon glowing above us in the starry night sky.

She reads me the first sentence, and I recite it wholeheartedly. "I vow my life." And the next. "I vow my forever."

Greyson sniffles, his cheeks burning bright red as Autumn feeds me the word. "I vow my soul."

"I vow my soul." My voice is thick with emotion as I complete the final phrase, feeling that door inside of me cracking open. "I bind myself to Greyson Gilmore from this night forward, for all of eternity."

Autumn removes her hands from our shoulders to our hands, one of hers on top and bottom, sandwiching them together. "I, Autumn Ashwood, honor this binding and unite these souls for eternity."

The door in my chest blows wide open, and my head flies back, my neck craning completely toward the sky.

Every cell in my body is vibrating like a mini earthquake is tearing through each one, building it back together with a piece of Greyson sewn inside.

I wince as the most blinding light erupts from our hands, growing brighter and engulfing all of us.

My mind calms uncontrollably as my body feels lighter than air, like I'm levitating off the ground.

Seconds, minutes, days pass me by as we float in this stream of light. The connection I felt to Greyson before is dying inside of me, the tether that tied us together cut in half.

Now, I don't have to tug on an invisible string to sense him. I can feel him as easily as I can feel myself, aware of his presence the way I'm aware that my feet are dangling above the pavement.

The light begins to dim, and we levitate back down to Earth, energy pulsing through me in waves, and it takes a moment for me to recognize that it's Greyson's, moving through me as freely as my own.

Forcing my eyes open, I take the deepest breath I ever have, the world around me feeling brand-new. The air is crisper, the colors sharper, like I'm seeing everything in ultra detail.

I feel invincible, like nothing could come close to challenging my strength. If I already feel like so much has changed within me, I can't imagine what Greyson is feeling right now.

His face is soft and relaxed, his eyes racing back and forth beneath his eyelids.

Brushing my thumbs against the silky soft skin of his hands, I stand up on my toes, whispering his name. "Greyson?"

He swallows hard before his eyes snap open, the blue of his irises more vibrant and brighter than ever. "This is...*incredible.*"

"Are you doing okay? I know it's probably a lot to adjust to," I warn him.

He chuckles, laughing in disbelief as his hands fall to my waist, and he lifts me with unnatural ease, spinning me around and holding me above his head.

"Oh my god, I love you so much!" Slowly lowering me back down, his face lights up. "I can feel you…your emotions. *Woah*. This is crazy. You feel this all of the time? How in the hell do you get anything done? How do you focus? It's like a new world has opened up inside of my mind."

Nodding, I can't help but smile and giggle at his exaggeration. "You'll learn to control it, but yes."

Running his hands through his hair, he then cups my face, his eyes bulging. "I can sense you, like I'm a compass and it's programmed to find you."

"I feel that too," I murmur, watching him experience the otherworldly sensations.

Autumn approaches us. "If you guys don't need anything from me, I will leave you to it. The ceremony is complete."

"Come here," I mumble, grabbing her arm and pulling her in for a hug, whispering in her ear, "Thank you."

She welcomes my embrace. "It truly was my honor."

Pulling away, Greyson hugs her quickly. "Thank you for everything, Autumn. You're one hell of a witch." He pauses, his face contorting with disbelief. "That's a sentence that I never thought I would say."

She laughs and dismisses herself with a finger wave, leaving us all alone.

Greyson's staring at his hands like they wield magical powers, but I suppose, in a way, his new strength does feel like that.

"I have one more surprise for you." His gaze flicks up through his lashes, catching me staring at him.

Rolling my eyes playfully, I step toward him, and he takes my hands, securing my arms around his neck. "Haven't you surprised me enough?"

He scrunches his eyes and nose. "*Never.*"

His fingertips trail along my arms, down my shoulders, and past my lower back until his hands cup my ass. He lifts me up, and I happily settle into one of my favorite places in the world…wrapped around his waist.

"Do you change your last names after ceremonies like this?" he asks, guiding us back down the aisle, up the stairs, and into our home.

"I think it is usually reserved for a more *human* ceremony. But if you want to change your last name to Barlowe, I certainly wouldn't have any qualms." I smirk, and he grins.

"Greyson Barlowe." He sounds it out, rolling it on his tongue. "I like it."

"Me too. It's hot, honestly," I murmur, purposefully making my voice smooth and sultry.

"Oh yeah? You think so?" He shrugs before declaring, "Then it's settled."

"Just like that?" I scoff as he crosses the foyer and ascends the marble staircase leading to the second floor.

His gaze falls to mine, and my heart skips a beat at the intensity in his stare. "I think you would find there isn't anything I wouldn't do to make you smile."

Gulping hard, I feel my blush spread down my neck and straight to my core. "I love you too."

He smiles. "Ms. Barlowe, what are your plans for the remainder of the night?"

My fangs tingle in my mouth, begging to join the party.

He chuckles. "Oh, I know that look."

Biting down on my cheek, I reel my willpower back in, my restraint hanging on by a thread.

As he walks through the threshold of our bedroom, I bat my eyelashes at him and whisper, "And what are you going to do about it?"

He carries me to the edge of the bed before lifting me up and tossing me down. Grabbing the heel of my right leg, he lifts it up, popping it off before nicely setting it on the ground, repeating the same steps with my other heel.

I gawk at him, enjoying the view as he undoes his belt, sliding it out of the loops and dropping it.

As he undoes the buttons of his shirt, he clears his

throat. "What was it you said you initially wanted from our arrangement? Feeding and fucking?"

Pointing at him, I add the missing f-word. "Don't forget frolicking."

He lifts his hands defensively and laughs. "Of course. How could I forget? My three favorite words."

Shimmying his shirt off his muscular shoulders, he peels the white sleeves off his defined arms, discarding the shirt to the floor.

The next to go is his pants, quickly joining his shirt on the ground. He pushes his boxers down, his throbbing erection calling out my name.

Grabbing onto my ankles, he lifts them slightly, and in one swift movement, he flips me over onto my stomach. Trailing his fingers up my legs and ass, he grabs the zipper of my dress and pulls it down slowly. His fingers hook into the thin straps on my shoulders, pulling them down as I press into the bed and hold myself up enough for him to peel the dress down my body, leaving me in nothing but red lace panties.

He crawls on top of me, his dick rubbing against my ass as his hands flatten against the bed on either side of my head, and he whispers into my ear, "I can feel your arousal right now, and *fuck*, it's intoxicating."

His tongue caresses the shell of my ear as he slaps his dick on my ass, earning a breathy gasp. "Please."

My senses are struggling to stay under control,

and I know the second I open them, they are going to be unbearably intense. Since the ceremony, everything has been heightened. Sight. Smell. Hearing. Taste.

I hesitate a second before opening myself up to Greyson, and my eyes roll to the back of my head from the overwhelming desire coursing through him.

"Please *what?*" he murmurs, nipping at my ear.

Rolling over, I look him straight in the eyes as I beg him. "Please fuck me."

"With pleasure, baby," he smirks, wrapping his fingers around my thigh and hiking my hip up, spreading me wide open. He glances between my legs. "Fuck, even through those panties, your pussy is so pretty."

My core pulses with his praise. Deciding to tap into my vamp speed, I tear the red lace apart.

"Goddamn," he murmurs before dropping between my legs and running his tongue through my wetness. "Mmm. So fucking sweet."

He sucks my clit into his mouth while easing two fingers inside of me, pumping me deliciously slow. But I want more. I'm not going to last long with how intense everything is, our emotions intertwining into a cloud of euphoria surrounding us.

"Greyson," I pant. "I need your cock. I need you

to fuck me." I feel his arousal spike, and I swear my pussy flutters in response.

Sitting up on his knees, he inches forward, pumping his thick cock from base to tip, the bead of precum shining in the dim light.

"So greedy," he groans, lining himself up.

I gasp as his tip slides in, stretching me around his girth as he rolls his hips, feeding me every inch. "For you? Always."

He freezes in place, breathing heavily. "I don't know where you begin and I end. I can feel your pleasure like it's my own. I've never been this high before. You're like a high that I'm going to chase every single day." He eases out and thrusts back into me, my head falling back.

He's right. This is otherworldly. Overwhelming in every sense, yet somehow not coming close to describing it.

It's like he's occupying my body as much as I am. My eyes struggle to stay open from the intensity as he picks his pace up, my moans becoming uncontrollable as my core begins to tighten up.

He growls. "Fuck, I'm not going to last very long like this. You feel too goddamn good, already tightening around me."

My mouth dries, thirsty and desperate to taste him, and he can sense my need, cocking his head to the side. Without hesitating, I sink my fangs into his neck, my eyes rolling to the back of my head as I drink from him.

"You suck me so good, baby. My blood is yours forever," he groans, and I'm done for.

Sliding a hand between my legs, he circles my clit, and my body explodes, fireworks igniting behind my eyelids as I scream out in ecstasy, "Greyson."

Running my fingers through his blond hair, I force my eyes open, meeting his desire-filled, hooded stare, and he moans before falling apart at the seams, buried in me to the hilt as his orgasm rocks through him in pulsing waves.

Epilogue
greyson

three months later

"What in the hell are you wearing?" Vivian cackles as she walks into the bedroom, bending over at the waist and laughing hysterically. "Greyson, *what* is that?"

Sliding off the bed, I hold my arms out to the side. "This old thing?" I give her a twirl. "A little custom T-shirt I ordered online."

She admires my black T-shirt with a printed image of Lulu and the words printed beneath the princess' photo: *proud cat daddy*.

"You're ridiculous!" She throws her head back as I proudly show off my new favorite shirt.

My laughter breaks free as I try to keep my tone serious and unwavering. "If you think that's crazy, then you're going to lose your mind when you see the shirt folded on the dresser behind you."

Her head snaps upright, her eyes widening and her jaw falling open. "You didn't."

Stretching my arms up, I glance behind her to the dresser. "Oh, but I did."

She spins around and grabs the shirt, unfolding it and holding it up. "Oh my god."

Hastily, she tears her sweater off and pulls the *proud cat mommy* shirt over her head. "A perfect fit, truly."

Her smile is uncontrollable, and she faces me, pure happiness radiating from her. "Thank you. I will cherish it always."

Stepping forward, I lean down and whisper, "What if I told you I have one more surprise?"

She studies me curiously, wondering what other tricks I have up my sleeve.

Reaching around her, I pull the drawer open and grab the little black box tucked inside. Her heart speeds up when she sees the black velvet, her face softening as I stand in front of her, my nerves spiking like crazy.

"*Greyson.*" My name breathlessly falls from her lips.

I can't contain my smile as I drop to one knee and stare up at the woman I am so incredibly in love with. In a way no one else in the world will ever possibly understand. We are a part of each other, our souls together as one.

She covers her mouth, her eyes welling up as I clear my throat. "I know it might not seem as significant as the Ceremony of Life and Death, but I want nothing more than to tie myself to you in every way possible. Will you do me the honor of being my wife?"

Dropping to her knees in front of me, she whimpers, "Yes, yes, of course I'll marry you."

Joy bubbles out of me as I pluck the gold-and-ruby engagement ring I had custom-made for her and slide it onto her left ring finger.

A tear slips past her lashes and rolls down her cheek as she studies her new ring in awe. "Greyson, it's so perfect. Oh my god, it's beautiful."

"I'm glad you like it. I got it made to match my own," I tell her, digging the gold-and-ruby wedding band from my pocket and slipping it onto my ring finger.

She squeals, holding her ring next to mine. "They're stunning together. A perfect pair."

Lulu meows loudly, announcing her arrival as she

jogs into the room. "Did I not mention that I also got Lulu a matching collar?"

Vivian chuckles, her face scrunching up. "You never cease to amaze me." She laughs and sits down on her ass, patting her lap, which Lulu happily jumps into. "This is actually so thoughtful."

She pets Lulu's black fur as she purrs loudly from the outpouring of love. "But we need to find you a few hobbies. Clearly, between the shirts, the jewelry and collar, you have too much time on your hands."

Rising to my feet, I offer her my hand and pull her up. "But I already have a few favorite hobbies."

"Oh, yeah? What are they?" She grins, popping her hand on her hip.

Swiping my tongue along my bottom lip, I decide to show her one of them, reaching out and grabbing her head, crashing my lips to hers, and kissing her tenderly.

As I pull away, her eyes stay shut as her cheeks flush, and she whispers, "That also happens to be one of my favorite hobbies. What else?"

Bending over, I throw her over my shoulder and walk the few steps to the bed, tossing her onto the soft mattress. "Do you want me to tell you or show you?"

She gulps, her lips parting. "I want you to show me."

Dropping onto the bed, I grab her pantyhose-covered knees, pushing them apart and finding she isn't wearing any panties. "When did you slip those off?"

I eye her curiously as she murmurs, a delicious smirk on her lips, "When you weren't looking when we got home and I could still feel your arousal pulsing."

"What? You just knew that I wouldn't be able to resist my favorite sweet treat?" Cocking my head to the side, my mouth waters as my gaze falls to her pretty pussy glistening in the light.

She bites down on her bottom lip and nods as I dip my head between her thighs and whisper, "You were right."

I flick my tongue out, dragging it through her soaking cunt. "Fuck, you taste so good." Savoring every second I get to have my face buried in her pussy, I worship her, sucking her clit into my mouth while finger fucking her to insanity.

"Greyson," she begs, my name a demand on her lips, and she doesn't need to say a word for me to know exactly what she wants.

She lifts her hips, and I strip the skirt from her legs, choosing to leave the sexy pantyhose and garter.

Grabbing the neck of my shirt, I pull it over my head and toss it onto the floor beside the bed, stripping my pants and boxers off as fast as possible.

Standing on my knees, I inch between hers, gripping my length in my hand, pumping myself back and forth as I hold her stare. "Is this what you want?"

She licks her lips, her eyes flickering red as she nods. "Yes." She lifts her hips up, and fuck if it isn't the hottest thing I've ever seen, her pussy begging for me."

Pressing my tip against her, I spit, watching it fall between us. Coating myself in it and her arousal, I push my tip inside her, earning a sharp gasp.

"Is that all you want?" I ask, demanding her to use her words and answer me. Fuck, there is something so intoxicating about having the powerful Vivian Barlowe at my whim.

"More, please," she whimpers, and when I don't give it to her immediately, she lifts her shirt off and unhooks her bra, tossing them aside. "Please."

Holding her lust-blown stare, I grab her hip and lift her right leg in the air, securing it over my shoulder. Anticipation looms in the air between us, electrifying every touch.

"Greyson," she whines, and I snap, giving her every inch she wants. In one smooth thrust, I fill her greedy cunt to the brim, my balls slapping against her ass.

"Fuckkk," I growl, overcome with pleasure.

Her hooded eyes, now completely red, hold

mine as her mouth falls open, exposing her two fangs. That sharp sting of pain when she first latches on makes everything that happens afterward better.

"You're mine, Vivian. All mine," I groan, rolling my hips into hers as her leg falls from my shoulder.

"Good." Her voice is powerful and sexy as hell, earning her another thrust.

Smirking, I lean down, hovering my lips over hers. "Care for a celebratory drink?"

Her eyes light up at my words, and she nods, wetting her lips.

"My blood only, forever," I tell her, my breath caressing her fangs.

She challenges me like she always does. "And if I drink from someone else?"

Chuckling darkly, I grab her chin firmly, calling her on her bluff. "You won't. Remember? You have *particular* tastes. How would you feel if I let someone else drink from me?" I push her frustration, a murderous jealousy unfurling from her.

"You saw what happened when someone did." She pulls from my grasp and sits up taller, holding a haunting kiss against my lips. "And I'll do it again. Because you're *mine*, Greyson."

Fuck, that's the hottest thing I've ever heard. I don't want to wait anymore, to draw it out any longer. I need her fangs in my neck while I show her just how happy I am to be hers.

Freezing, I can't help but think about how fucking lucky I am to spend forever with her.

She pouts and wiggles her hips. "Greyson. Do you want me to beg you? Because I will. I need you so badly right now. Please, for the love of —"

Sealing my lips against hers, I cut her off, plunging my tongue into her mouth, and as I pull away, I playfully murmur against her fangs, "Shut up and bite me."

Red spider veins extend beneath her eyes as I physically watch her willpower snap in half. She grabs my neck, cocking it to the side at the same time I ease out of her.

She punctures my neck, and I slam into her. I fuck her relentlessly as she drinks greedily from my neck. We continue to worship each other as we crest the edge of euphoria, our bodies winding up together.

She releases my neck, blood trailing down the side of her O-shaped lips as she tightens around me, moaning my name repeatedly. Grabbing her hand, I lock my fingers in hers and pin it above her head as we fall apart at the seams, wrapped in each other's embrace.

Nothing could have prepared me for the changes I would go through after the ceremony of Life and Death. How intensely everything around me would change.

My strength was something I prided myself on before, but it was nothing compared to the strength and power that flows through me now.

Seeing the world through the lens of Vivian's gaze has been nothing short of enlightening and life-altering.

Feeling her presence and her emotions has only deepened the love I have for her, rooting it deep in my bones. She didn't just change my life; she gave me life, ripping me from the life I never truly wanted and placing the world in my hands.

I'm not just faster and stronger. I heal almost instantly, the same way her body does. My sense of smell is totally different, every scent more intense. It's like my senses have become supernatural. I can smell people's scent before they even turn into our driveway.

I no longer have a need for my glasses; my vision is better than it ever could have been as a human. I can see details on the dust particles floating through the air. I can see the perspiration on my skin.

It's like I've been living in a blurry world and I just got upgraded to high definition, seeing details that I never knew existed.

But as high as the highs are, the lows hit just as hard.

Today is Cheryl's birthday, and every year since her passing, I've brought flowers to her grave and had lunch with her. Whether rain, sun, or snow, I have never missed it. Today won't be any different, except I'll get to introduce her to Vivian.

We're stopping into Ambrose Floral Shop before we head to the cemetery to get the prettiest bundle of flowers for the prettiest gal.

"Welcome in!" The same lady who was working the last time I was here greets us from the cooler, loading new stems into the white buckets.

"Hello!" Vivian greets her, trailing her hand on one of the house plants, caressing the leaf tenderly.

The nice lady shuts the glass door of the cooler and turns to face us, brushing her hair out of her face. "Two dozen red roses." She points at me. "I remember you. What can I help you with today?"

Vivian smirks at the mention of the roses, and I almost break, laughing at the memory, but I manage to hold it together.

"We need a bouquet of flowers—primarily pink if possible. It was her favorite color." An image of Cheryl wearing one of her pink sweaters flashes in my mind, my chest contracting at the pain that follows.

Vivian walks over to me calmly, resting her hand on my arm, offering me comfort both from her touch and her emotion that sinks into my chest, soothing the ache.

"Absolutely. Give me a few minutes, and I'll get a bouquet put together for you."

"Thank you," I murmur before she gets to work, grabbing stems of different flowers from the coolers.

Before I know it, she has created the most perfect bundle, one that I know would bring a happy tear to Cheryl's eyes.

God, I wish she were still here. I may have stumbled down a different path than the one we planned together, but I know she would be so proud that I'm following my heart.

The little time we had together, that is all she ever wanted me to do—to focus on the good and allow myself to love and be loved. So many people—countless, really—showed me firsthand the evils that exist in this world.

They aren't always monsters with fangs; they are a seemingly normal man named Alfred who welcomes you into his home and beats you behind closed doors. They are a woman named Monica who puts locks on the fridge and pantry doors, using food as a tool for punishment, starving a six-year-old child so consistently that they are too weak to leave their bed.

Cheryl was the one good exception to the horrors of my experience in foster care. She gave me a second chance at life, giving me the tools I needed to succeed.

I regret not getting to know her deeper, not asking her questions about her childhood, her marriage to her late husband, and everything I could have learned that I'll never get the chance to know now.

But it's funny because when you're young, you never think of the lives your parents lived before they had you. They are just mom or dad, and you're too focused on your own lives to dig into their past. Only when you start to experience life, truly live through the highs and the lows, do you wonder what tribulations they may have faced and overcome.

But that regret is one I will live with for eternity. And I will have to accept that I was blessed enough to know Cheryl at all.

We pay for the flowers and head to the cemetery, my heart in my throat as I visit my oldest friend.

Hours pass by with ease, and before we know it,

we've spent the entire afternoon hanging out with Cheryl, reminiscing on old stories that I know would've had Cheryl laughing up a storm. It was nice spending that time with my two favorite ladies, not including Lulu beans, of course.

I can't help but wonder what the old Greyson would be doing right now if he never took a chance to hang out with two classmates heading to a bar one random night.

One thing's for certain: I wouldn't be bonded to a vampire named Vivian who owns me, heart and soul. And god, what a shame that would be.

We have to stop at the Barlowe on our way back home. Vivian said she has to talk to Ava about something, and I'm happy to tag along.

Surprisingly, this is only my second time at Vivian's hotel, and I have such a different point of view looking at it now, knowing what lies inside and beneath the surface.

As we walk up the few steps to the entrance, the doorman pulls it open, greeting Vivian. "Ms. Barlowe. Welcome."

"Thank you, Greg." She smiles, passing through the door with me following closely behind.

Guests wander through the grand foyer, some even enjoying time sitting on the benches around the sky-high clock tower. Little do they know what happens down below.

Vivian leads me to a locked double-door entrance, pressing her thumb onto the little screen that scans her fingerprint, the door clicking unlocked a second later.

"Fancy," I murmur as she pushes the thick wooden door open and we step through, the lock securing back in place the second it swings shut.

She turns and faces me, walking backward and holding her hands out for me to grab, and I happily slide my hands around hers.

I can feel the sense of surprise building inside of her. I guess that's a downfall of being able to sense each other's feelings. It's like a language all of its own.

She sighs, her eyes locking onto mine as I feel disappointment trickle into her. "I was doing so good keeping the surprise a secret."

Chuckling, I drop one of her hands before pulling her into my side with our still-connected hand, intertwining my fingers with hers. "Don't beat yourself up. I still don't know exactly what we're doing here."

She nods, coming to a halt and turning to face a large wooden door. Standing behind her, I rub my hands up and down her arms as another scanner reads her thumb, the door unlocking once approved.

She opens the door to find the members of the High Council sitting in wingback chairs around a circular table, two of the chairs still empty.

They welcome us with cheer and hugs before finding their seats. Vivian sits in one of the empty chairs, gesturing to me to sit down beside her in the other free seat.

The members smile at me, and I can feel the same waves of eager anticipation billowing off them.

Vivian sets her hand on top of mine, pulling my attention. "As all of you know, with Jason's passing, we have the duty of finding that special individual to fill his spot on the High Council." She pauses and looks up at me. "You have shown bravery beyond measure and selflessness to protect those around you at all costs. You are genuine and kind. All traits held in high regard. Because of that, we would like to offer the seat to you."

My chest warms, my heart racing at their offer.

"Will you accept?" she asks, hope blossoming in her like a garden of flowers.

Glancing at each of the faces around the table, I nod, knowing that in this seat, I'll be able to make a difference, have an impact on the world that matters. "Yes, of course, I accept."

Everyone claps, their words of kindness filling the room at my acceptance.

"We are lucky to have you." Ava smiles, sitting beside Vivian.

My gratitude is almost too much to bear that they offered me a seat at this table. "Thank you, guys, from the bottom of my heart."

"That settles that," Vivian declares, sliding her chair back and rising to her feet. "Quickest meeting ever."

"This was the only reason you needed to stop in?" I ask her, surprised at how well she actually managed to keep it from me.

She nods, biting down on her bottom lip. "I'm sorry. Forgive me. I was so excited it was almost impossible to rein that in anytime we spoke about the council."

Standing to my feet, I kick the chair back and offer her my hand. "I forgive you."

She slides her fingers in mine and stands to her feet, and I can't help myself from scanning her head to toe.

Besides, I have a surprise up my own sleeve.

"I suppose we do have one more announcement," she swoons and hold her hand in the air, showing off her ring.

Ooos and ahhs ripple through the room as they congratulate us. Endless hugs going around.

My fingers brush against the thin pantyhose just

beneath her brown suede skirt as she crosses in front of me. I've torn so many pairs apart that she started buying the ones that are thigh-high, secured in place by a garter belt.

She looks good today. I mean, fuck, she looks perfect every day. But her hair up in that sexy loose bun and those long legs are calling out my name.

We say our goodbyes and Vivian squeezes my hand tightly, and I know she can tell exactly what I'm thinking or rather feeling. And I don't try to hide it in the slightest.

We wander down the hallway and out of the first secured door we pass through.

"Holy shit. I think that's…" I pause, studying the guy across the lobby before calling out, "Ethan!"

He whips around, his face lighting up as his gaze lands on us. He jogs over to us. "Greyson, what's up?"

Dropping my stare to Vivian, I smirk. "Just stopping in for a few things. What have you been up to?" It dawns on me that we are standing in the Barlowe, the place we first met. "Wait, what are you doing here?"

He chuckles nervously, rubbing the back of his neck. "About that…I, umm, met someone."

Listening to his heart, it's pounding in his chest, his breathing kicking up. "Oh yeah, who's the lucky girl?"

His freckled cheeks flush. "Well, you actually know her—"

A sweet, familiar voice calls out from behind us, cutting him off. "There are you!"

Ava.

Lightly slapping Ethan's shoulder, I scoff. "You could have told me you're seeing Ava. I should have known, honestly."

"Yeah?" He laughs. "With all your new Spidey senses?" He scoffs, mocking me playfully.

"Yeah, exactly with those." I smile as Ava walks up to us, sliding her arm around Ethan's waist as he throws his arm around her shoulders. "You guys look good together."

"That is the sweetest compliment." Ava swoons, her hand pressing against her heart.

"After everything with Victor, she helped me get through the aftermath." Panic spreads in him at the mention of his attacker. "She kept me sane."

"Good. But you know, Ava, I've become rather protective of Ethan here," I tease. "Remember your motto."

Ava rolls her eyes and dismisses me. "Don't be ridiculous. I would never hurt Ethan."

Her heart rate is steady, and she means every word. "I know you won't."

She glares at me. "Don't tap into my emotions. I

think I liked you better when you didn't have your abilities."

Vivian bursts out laughing. Tugging her hand, I pull her along with me, waving at Ava and Ethan as we stride away. "We will catch you guys later. Ethan, call me if she gives you any trouble."

He nods, side-eyeing Ava, and I would be concerned if I couldn't feel the happiness radiating off him.

"You want to be on the council, right? Not just because I put you on the spot in front of a room full of people?" Vivian asks me as we cross through the foyer and descend down the stairs outside.

"You overestimate your peer pressure skills, love," I joke, and she glares up at me through her lashes. "Of course I want to be a part of it. The work that you do is important. It makes a real difference in the world."

Her shoulders relax, and she grins. "Okay, I was just checking." She gasps. "Oh, we need to get you some custom suits made. Ugh, you are going to look so goddamn good in a suit."

"You can play dress-up with me all day long, baby." I throw my arm around her shoulders and pull her into my side. "Now, let's go home. I'm starving, and I'm sure you could use a little pick-me-up."

She flicks her stare up at me, flashing her red eyes for just a second. "You know me so well."

"Although, I should really cut you off. You have to have gotten your fill for the next six months. Surely, you would be just fine without another drop."

She has a love and hate relationship when I play hard to get with her. She wants control, to chase me and bend me to her will, and I happily play along, as long as she begs me for it.

"You love when I feed on you, and you know it!" She gasps,

Grabbing her jaw, I pull her to me and claim her lips with mine. "I can't help it. I love everything when it comes to you."

As we hit the pavement outside, I shudder at the cool breeze that whips in the air around us. Saint Eldritch became my home in more ways than I could have ever predicted. I lived here for years without realizing the secrets hiding in plain sight. But I can see everything clearly now. Any doubt I had regarding what I wanted out of life is long gone. I've never been more certain that where I am is right where I belong.

Vivian holds her palm up, and I thread my fingers in hers. "I love you, Greyson."

"I love you too," I murmur, leaning down and kissing the forehead of the girl I was born to love.

Thank you for reading Shut Up and Bite Me! If you enjoyed it, please leave a review on Amazon and Goodreads!

Want to read more from Pru Schuyler? Check out her backlist below!

Nighthawks Series (new adult pro hockey romance)
Find Me in the Rain
Find Me on the Ice
Find Me Under the Stars
Not My Coach
Find Me in the Fire

Mrs. Claus Standalone Duet (adult holiday romance)
Stealing Mrs. Claus
Becoming Mrs. Claus

Wicked Series (young adult mystery/suspense romance)
The Wicked Truth
The Wicked Love
The Wicked Ending

Saint Eldritch Series (paranormal romance)
Shut Up and Bite Me

about the author

Pru Schuyler is a Top 10 Amazon Best-Selling author, best known for her Nighthawks hockey romance series. She writes *happily ever afters to cry for*, including characters and stories that her readers can truly empathize with. At the heart, her books focus on undying love.

She secretly judges people who get through the day without any caffeine because she consumes an insane amount in order to function. She lives in the Midwest with her adored fur babies and husband. When she isn't getting lost in her writing, she is busy procrastinating by attending her local NAHL games, watching her favorite shows and movies, and spending time with her family at home.

Printed in Great Britain
by Amazon